Strictly
CONFIDENTIAL

Strictly
CONFIDENTIAL

A JAZZY LOU NOVEL

Roxy Jacenko

ALLEN&UNWIN
SYDNEY · MELBOURNE · AUCKLAND · LONDON

First published in 2012

Allen & Unwin
Sydney, Melbourne, Auckland, London

83 Alexander Street
Crows Nest NSW 2065
Australia
Phone: (61 2) 8425 0100
Fax: (61 2) 9906 2218
Email: info@allenandunwin.com
Web: www.allenandunwin.com

Cataloguing-in-Publication details are available
from the National Library of Australia
www.trove.nla.gov.au

ISBN 978 1 74237 757 5

Typeset in 12.2/18.5 Joanna MT Std by Bookhouse, Sydney
Printed and bound in Australia by the SOS Print + Media Group.

10 9 8 7 6 5 4 3 2

Part
ONE

1

It all began with knickers. And, like any good outfit should, this story ends in knickers too. But not just any knickers. We're talking luxurious artisan lingerie from Vixenary's Sabotage collection. Knickers that are one hundred percent silk with stylish soutache embellishment. Knickers to make you a pin-up when you're stripped down. Knickers that are on trend, not off the rack. And in a g-string, naturally.

This is Sydney, after all.

We may be close, here in the Emerald City, to the great fashion capitals of the world (materially if not geographically), but we're not averse to a little flashiness, to a little gratuitous baring of flesh. So it's fitting, really, that my glittering career as Sydney's premier fashion publicist was launched with the elastic of a size-zero g-string.

If this were elsewhere in Australia, say the Apple Isle, my start would probably have come in the form of a kitsch pair of undies tastelessly plastered with an invitation to view my map of Tassie. Or, if my life as a PR doyenne began, as many do, in that other apple – the Big Apple – I'd probably be talking DKNY spandex briefs. Hip and urban and taking no shit, yeah? Unlike in London, where they'd be sensible charmeuse panties parading as your nanny's knickers or whatever other campaign Agent Provocateur dreamed up to shift smalls to repressed Poms. Or Paris, where I'd be clad in some exquisite Chantal Thomass creation, only to bend over and have it ripped off by the marauding French press, as any PR girl would willingly do.

Metaphorically speaking, of course.

Perhaps, if my life as a publicist had begun in Milan, I'd be lounging in my La Perla finest, all *frastaglio* embroidery and mixing it with Italy's beautiful people. Hell, I'd probably have found myself at one of Berlusconi's bunga-bunga parties in the name of product placement where I'd thank God that, in my twenties, I was far too old to be his type.

Instead, it all began with a red Vixenary g-string in the back-streets of Sydney's Darlinghurst.

'OMG! Emergency!' her voice shrieked from my BlackBerry as I answered my phone in my sleep.

My dream slid to the floor and lay dead among the detritus beside my bed. Mangled Manolos, last month's *Muse* magazine, an overdue press release and now an interrupted dream: it was like a graveyard down there.

Admittedly, I was only dreaming of being somewhere loud and dizzyingly disorienting with my boyfriend, Will. That could have been us at Paddington Inn any old Tuesday night. Hell, we were probably about set to launch into an argument over: a) ridiculous working hours (mine); b) ridiculous partying hours (his); or c) the fact we need Facebook face-recognition software to identify each other these days. Eyes closed or open. It's not like it was a dream of being locked in Chanel's flagship store on rue Cambon after-hours while a reincarnated Coco Chanel crafted a bespoke version of her iconic tweed suit for me and Karl Lagerfeld fed me Ladurée macaroons by hand. Hypothetically, say.

Wait, was someone on the phone? Talking in rhymes? In the middle of the night? Was Dr Seuss on the line?

'Sorry, who is this?' I said, rubbing at my eyes.

My bedside clock said 3.12 am. Glaringly.

'It's Diane! OMG!' the phone said. Piercingly.

Diane Wilderstein of Wilderstein PR was my boss and the only person over twenty-five to use OMG without irony.

She went on: 'Raven is completely off her face at Kit and Kaboodle and the paps are out front waiting for a money shot. I'm still in Melbourne so you'll have to sort this. Now!'

Frantically blinking sleep from my eyes, I tried to process what the hell was happening. Kit and Kaboodle, yes? Rue Cambon, non?

I turned on the light. Ouch! Bad idea.

'Where do you want me to go?' I managed eventually.

Diane sighed, as if even from interstate my ineptitude was draining. 'Kit and *Kaboodle* nightclub in Kings Cross!' she repeated. 'Raven's fallen off the fucking wagon and if the paps get a picture of her we're fucked. Gone. Kaput!'

I appreciated her spelling out the severity of the situation, I really did, but as it was, a 3 am wake-up call had done the trick. Butterflies started flittering around my stomach. The kind of butterflies usually reserved for monumental occasions. Like a bat mitzvah. Or a first date. Or the first precious minutes of a Sass & Bide stocktake clearance.

'Get there *now*,' Diane demanded. 'Are you at home?'

'Yes,' I whispered and immediately regretted my honesty. I should have lied and said I was staying at a friend's in Palm Beach or somewhere equally isolated. That way I could have bought myself a few more precious minutes under my doona.

'Thank God. Paddington isn't far from the Cross so you can be there in ten minutes. Call me as soon as you find Raven. Do you understand?'

'Yes,' I answered, dragging my arse out of bed and my trackies from the floor, before slipping them straight over my satin pyjama shorts.

Diane, however, didn't wait to hear my answer. She'd already hung up the phone and, with it, any chance I had of returning to sleep. My work fate was sealed.

If I'm honest though, my work fate had been sealed long before Diane dialled my digits that night. In just the same way that some kids are destined to follow their parents' vocational footsteps into law or dentistry or chartered accounting, I trod like a lemming the well-worn track laid down by my parents. The path, that is, of plain old hard work.

Perhaps it was because both my parents came from housing commission neighbourhoods more rat-infested than a Ksubi catwalk and then clawed their way up from there that I found myself inheriting one hell of a serious work ethic. If mine is a rags to riches story, those riches haven't come without hard slog. First my parents' and then mine.

Or perhaps it was because Mum and Dad threw every cent they slavishly earned into a very expensive Jewish private-school education for me that I embraced my lot as a minion in the marketplace so wholeheartedly. After all, nothing teaches you to suck it up and work hard, princess, like six years of orthodox education. Then again, maybe it was the copy of Donald Trump's autobiography, *The Art of the Deal*, which my grandmother Bubbe gave me for my tenth birthday that really set me on the course of career conscientiousness. (Not to mention a lifetime of megalo-mania.) Or it could have been the fact that my parents and Bubbe talked of nothing but business strategy at the dinner table each night. I could talk shop with them or I could not talk at all. And that's not much of a choice for a teenage girl.

I got my first job during high school, first at Bondi Junction McDonald's scooping fries, and then scrubbing walls at the local florist, and finally printing pics of Eastern Suburbs identities at Kodak. In fact, the more I think about it, the more I'm sure this last job was responsible for more than just lining my Dollarmite account with pocket money, because it was here that I first developed photos of visiting Hollywood stars and, with them, most likely, my passion for PR.

So even though I came from the wrong side of the PR tracks, what I lacked in connections and social standing I more than made up for with diligence and dogged hard work. The kind of diligence that enabled a person to survive four years working for Diane Wilderstein. Because if the devil wears Prada then Diane keeps Miuccia in business. I swear that woman is Lucifer in luxury labels.

Yes, I had the kind of tenacity that saw a person progress from receptionist to office-coordinator-slash-personal-assistant-to-Diane and then, finally, to the role of senior publicist at Wilderstein PR. Although the title was purely semantics: what my day-to-day working life at Wilderstein really entailed was being at the mercy of Diane's every whim. Run a media campaign for a famous fashion label or run to the drycleaners to collect Diane's laundry. Whip up a press release or whip up a batch of cupcakes for Diane's client meeting. Look after a celeb's media tour in Sydney or look after Diane's caffeine habit. Devise a publicity schedule for a major international organisation or devise a way to get the latest Birkin design into Diane's possession before COB. I did it all.

In short, I was cursed with the kind of diligence that would make a person think nothing of dragging herself out of bed at three-thirty on a Thursday morning to track down a totalled client before they did serious harm to their reputation.

A thousand thoughts raced through my mind as I battled to get out the door. Most of them incoherent and certainly none of them printable.

I focused on trying to approximate clothed. Trackies? Check. EMU ugg boots? Check. T-shirt? Fuck. The first top I laid my hands on bore a slogan that read *Desperate Housewives Season Five, March 2005: Juicy!* It was hardly a to-the-minute sartorial selection but who cared? Who was I likely to see at Kit and Kaboodle before dawn on a Thursday morning? Aside from Raven, of course. I'd better bloody see her there.

Now, handbag? Kitchen table. Makeup bag? In bag. Phone? Bed. Got it. Go!

A text came through from Diane just as I picked up my phone: *Are you there yet?* it screamed and I tripped down the front stairs reading it. Bolting outside I scanned for taxis and replied to Diane: *Sure. Almost.*

I willed a taxi to appear.

Nothing. Only the monotonous drone of cicadas.

Shit.

At this point I decided the best course of action was to leg it. This was a rash decision. Still, avoiding death-by-Diane was a powerful motivator and soon my legs were pounding down Oxford Street. When suddenly it came to me: no bra.

It seemed the homeless man perched nearby on his pile of plastic bags worked this out before I did. 'Juicy,' he muttered croakily as I scuffed past in my EMU uggs, my trench dangling off one shoulder, my left breast completely visible through the white promo tee.

Enjoy, mate, I thought grimly.

And then, was that a taxi? A taxi! With its light on? Yes!

The cab sped up on approach and hastily pulled in. Hurrah! I dived onto the backseat and slammed the door behind me.

'Darlinghurst-Road-Kings-Cross-quick-as-you-can-please,' I said, beyond breathless.

The driver turned around and was staring at me open-mouthed, his cab stationary at the kerb. What? Had no one seen a bra-less woman in Paddington until tonight?

'Go!' I shouted, flicking up the collar of my coat in a vain attempt at some dignity and he put his foot to the floor.

Resting my head against the taxi window, I turned my attention to the PR disaster at hand. Surely I was not the only person who had seen this coming? I mean, even as a senior publicist I was still only a nonentity in the galaxy of Public Relations. A mere red dwarf. Far-flung and unimportant and straining to feel the warmth of the sun's rays from the outer rim of the media Milky Way. And given PR itself was considered only one small spiral galaxy in the vast fashion universe, I cannot understate my insignificance. The (working) dog star of the universe, that was me. But pleb or not, even I could see getting Raven out to Australia had been a big mistake from the start.

Only eight months earlier the entire globe had been glued to Raven's spectacular downfall as she'd plummeted from US pop starlet to prescription pill-popping junkie overnight, thanks to a rogue YouTube clip. In the clip, Raven crawled around someone's backyard on all fours looking for her lost bag of cocaine, wearing nothing but a cheap g-string. While the coke was unarguably lost, all signs as to where it might have gone pointed to the streams of blood pouring from Raven's nostrils. Naturally, the video was an instant viral sensation when it appeared online in twelve easy-to-use chapters, each named artfully for the on-camera quotes in each clip. My personal favourite was 'Where the fark is ma shit?' but 'Who's cravin' some Raven?' was also soaring up YouTube's 'Most viewed' list. In fact, if only her latest music single 'Trespass' had got that many hits, Raven could have retired right now.

The upside of two hundred million people viewing Raven in her knickers was that her infamous derrière now fit perfectly the, ahem, brief for the new Vixenary underwear campaign. The downside was Vixenary was one of our key clients so I had to deal with all Raven's shit. You see, Vixenary had just released their Sabotage collection of very risqué, very expensive g-strings which carried the advertising line: *It's all you ever need.* A claim Raven had adroitly proved by her choice of attire in her YouTube clips, making her Vixenary's model muse. Why the ill-advised Raven saw spruiking smalls as the obvious next step on her path to a redeemed public profile, I couldn't tell you. But as to our side of the bargain? Easy. Raven was broke after literally blowing her bucks, so she came tantalisingly cheap. Which was how I found myself hurtling towards Kings Cross at 3.30 am, sporting pyjama shorts under a pair of tracksuit pants, in order to retrieve Raven.

Still, I was confused. Raven had been in town for two days now and besides all the predictable diva demands, the kid had turned out to be all right. Straight even (well, most of the time). From OBs (outdoor broadcasts) on Show FM, to in-store signings for Vixenary intimates, from morning TV performances to evening prime time,

Raven hadn't caused me, as her minder, a single headache – until now. In fact, the only blip on her charge sheet since Monday had been her suspiciously dilated pupils and unaccountable twitchiness when on stage at Westfield centre court, Bondi Junction. A twitchiness that couldn't *quite* be explained away by having to front a crowd of hip-thrusting, booty-gyrating tweens. Although, granted, that was enough to make anyone jumpy.

Could it be that Diane had been given the wrong information? Had Raven really flown the coop? Is it possible Diane was sending me out on a wild-goose chase in the middle of the night? And if so, was it really a mistake or some perverted fun on her part? After all, the woman fired publicists like normal people got spray tans. Who knew what she did for kicks after hours.

Pulling up outside the club, I saw with a sinking heart that Diane wasn't wrong. Four photographers lined the footpath, shooting the breeze with who I assumed was the owner of the club (and most likely the one who had alerted them). Due to the hour, and the fact it was midweek, there was no one on the door when I schlepped inside, leaving me free to run upstairs to the second level in the sixties-inspired club, all vintage furniture and black and white patterned carpet, where I began searching for our pill-popping protégée.

It didn't take long to find her.

There, in a corner near the dance floor, was Raven. She was flicking her head as though trapped in a beehive, and her bottom jaw looked like it was about to detach and go and get a cocktail.

I stalked over. 'Raven, hi. Remember me? Jasmine? I'm the publicist who's been looking after you for the past few days,' I said to the hot mess.

'Someone has been, like, cutting off my fucking hair,' she said by way of reply, still flicking her hair and ferociously licking her lips.

Aside from the sweat beads forming on her forehead, both Raven and her allegedly hacked-off hair looked fine to me.

'What the fuck have they done?' she shouted, looking around for the rogue hairdresser while pulling long blonde locks out herself.

People were starting to stare. This kid was attracting way too much attention here. Bloody Hollywood exhibitionist; she couldn't go anywhere without demanding an audience.

Nervous about potentially catching something from touching her, I reached out and removed her hands from her head, where she was fast giving herself alopecia. Next, I brought my face up close to hers and spoke loudly and clearly, trying to avoid any polysyllabic words: 'Look, you are fine and you are hot. In fact, why don't we go to the bathroom so you can see for yourself?'

Raven smiled and nodded enthusiastically.

Grabbing her hand, I wheeled her around and was pointing out the direction of the bathrooms when I spotted her handbag lying nearby. It was a caramel Balenciaga behemoth that I'd drooled over just the day before. I snatched up the tote and dragged Raven towards the toilets when an 'I Kissed a Girl' megamix boomed from the dance floor.

'Wooooo! Katy Perry is a pimp!' Raven screamed, skipping and waving her free hand in the air.

Ushering her into the bathroom, I felt the butterflies in my stomach subside for the first time since Diane's phone call. I could cross item one off my to-do list: I'd managed to locate Raven. Now all I had to do was smuggle her out of here. First, however, I'd need to scoop her up off the bathroom floor where she'd fallen over and was lying sprawled on the wet, toilet paper-strewn tiles. Shit.

I fantasised briefly about the YouTube sensation this scene would create if I filmed it. Not to mention the price I could fetch from the tabloids if I whipped out my camera-phone right now. If shots of Britney Spears and her lover Jason Trawick in Australia scored snappers fifty thousand dollars as reported, surely a coked-up Raven spread all over a bathroom floor could cover my rent for the rest of the year? Tempting. But then, so was remaining gainfully employed, so I cast the idea out of my mind.

Eventually vertical, Raven looked to me for direction, so I led her to an empty toilet cubicle where I flipped the lid down, plonked her on top, locked the door and breathed out heavily. In front of me sat my diva-cum-detainee. This was not what I had planned for my night. Raven, meanwhile, snatched her handbag from my wrist and started riffling through it.

'Where the fark is ma shit?' she said, almost pitch-perfect to her YouTube video. Could this be the first time this kid had performed without lip-syncing?

I ignored her, knowing full well that if there was any coke left Raven would have been licking it out of the satchel when I arrived.

So what now? Our Vixenary cover girl could hardly just walk out of there. Hell, she could hardly walk full stop. We were in the middle of Kit and Kaboodle, in the heart of Sydney's bustling Kings Cross; there was no back door and, on a quiet Thursday morning, the paps would simply wait it out until Raven appeared. And of course, carrying her out was out of the question. Much as I wanted publicity for my client, I didn't want it in a Kate Moss kinda way.

I checked the clock on my phone. It was almost 4 am now and the club would be shutting in an hour. My BlackBerry had been going off as wildly and regularly as Raven's hair flicks with calls and texts from Diane but I hadn't answered any of them. Instead I focused on Raven. She needed water and lots of it if I was to get her to a magazine shoot at 10 am later today.

'Where the fark is ma shit?' Raven interrupted, still looking in her bag.

'Outside,' I lied. 'If you promise to stay here I'll go and get it.' I spoke to her like I was speaking to a small child.

'Promise,' she responded in kind.

I went and found an ATM in the club and withdrew two hundred dollars from my work float. I was on my way back to the bathroom when a random chick stopped me. 'OMFG! Are you Raven?' she asked, just as off her head as the diva herself.

'No,' I said, battling to hide my disgust. Just what I needed, to be confused for a Hollywood wannabe. As if wandering round the Cross in my trackies wasn't embarrassment enough.

'You two totally look alike,' she said and I hurried off considering plastic surgery.

Returning to the toilets with three bottles of water, I was relieved to find Raven where I'd left her.

'Did you find any coke?' She looked up hungrily.

'Sure, there's some in the water,' I said. 'Drink up. I'm getting more now.'

She started gulping down the water.

Staring at the drugged-up diva in front of me, I realised the chick outside was kinda right. We did look vaguely similar. Although Raven was slightly shorter than me (she was barely my height when she was in heels), we were roughly the same size with shoulder-length blonde hair. The only difference was hers was wavy and more golden, whereas mine was straight and lighter blonde. Our faces, however, were so completely different we could never be considered lookalikes. Happy days. Coked-up Cate was just hallucinating.

And then, of course, it hit me.

Propping Raven up, I started undressing her, desperately hoping she wouldn't remember this in the morning. Clearly inspired by Katy Perry's lyrics, and perhaps assuming I was undressing her because I found her irresistible, she tried to kiss me. But as flattering as that was, I doggedly kept going.

'Fine then,' she sulked.

Five minutes later I had managed to switch our outfits completely and I sat her back down, took her BlackBerry and logged onto my own Twitter account.

'Raven, I'm going to find you some more coke. You have to promise me you won't leave the bathroom though, okay? Here, you can go online and see what everyone is doing back home. Talk to your friends.'

She snatched the phone without saying anything.

'Don't leave,' I stressed.

Whipping out of my bag a pocket-sized can of Schwarzkopf hairspray I went to the basin, wet my hair and gave myself an eighties quiff like hers. I also squeezed into her lilac-coloured Christian Louboutins which were at least one size too small. My feet hurt immediately.

Once again outside the bathroom, I looked around the club until I spotted the nearest drug dealer, instantly recognisable by the fact he was wearing sunglasses inside and was carrying a bumbag.

I went straight up to him. 'How much for your sunglasses?' I asked.

'Say what?' he replied.

'I'll give you fifty bucks for your sunnies.'

'Don't you want some gear, darlin?'

'No, just the glasses, please.' I smiled.

'These are my Dolces, man. They were over five hundred bucks,' he said loudly, looking around to see who had heard.

D&G is probably the easiest label to identify as a fake. Imitation branding is always much more square than the font for the real Italian stuff. These were more square than the gold caps on the guy's teeth.

'A hundred bucks, cash, right now,' I said.

'Okay,' he said without hesitating.

I handed over the money and grabbed the sunnies, which had been shielding pupils the size of dinner plates.

Walking down the main staircase my butterflies returned with a vengeance. *How the hell do I get myself into these situations?* I wondered. Less than an hour ago I was lying blissfully unconscious in bed. Now I was battling to balance in a pair of too-tight Louboutins while being weighed down with a Balenciaga handbag the size of the average family car, and all as I tried to impersonate a celebrity who I was holding captive in a nightclub toilet. I felt duplicitous, demoralised, downright out of my depth. And all in an outfit I never would have chosen. This must be what a bridesmaid feels like at a wedding they're not quite in favour of. Only worse, because at some point during the nuptials I seemed to have stepped into the bride's shoes. I tried to concentrate on putting one squished foot in front of the other.

As I tottered towards the door of the club, people began to titter. Eyes bored into me as heads swung in my direction. 'Raven!' someone called. I tried to walk faster. 'Hey, Raven!' the voice came again. I pressed on. 'Raven!' they persisted as other voices joined the chorus. I put my head down and kept ploughing across the nightclub, faster than any shotgun wedding. My feet ached with every step. This whole 'something borrowed' malarkey was not my bag.

Then, just as I was gaining some ground across the beer-soaked carpet, I hit a snag. A big snag. A snag in the form of the random who had accosted me earlier in the night and accused me of looking like Raven. Only this time she had a point.

'Wow! Raven!' she cooed, stepping in front of me and blocking my already precarious path. 'I can't believe you're here. In Sydney!'

I smiled grimly. I couldn't believe I was there either. 'Hey everyone, it's Raven!'

Before I could stop her, my groupie turned and announced my star-studded presence to anyone who might just have missed it. I instinctively ducked my head, but there was no stopping my number one fan.

'OMG. Raven, will you sing for us?' she shrieked. Her friends cheered in support. It was like one big pop-star love-in. I half-expected Clover Moore to jump out from behind a pillar and offer me the keys to the city. Of course, spying our middle-aged Lord Mayor in a Kings Cross nightclub at four in the morning was about as likely as me giving an impromptu performance of Raven's back catalogue.

Waving my hands to get the attention of my growing legion of fans, I shook my head regretfully. 'Sorry!' I whispered, pointing an index finger to my neck. 'Sore throat!' They looked downcast. This alone made me feel perversely upbeat. I waved again before continuing on my trek to the doorway.

Hesitating on the threshold, I pushed my hair forward one last time in a lame attempt to hide my face, before stepping onto the street outside.

Cue: pandemonium.

The paps that were lounging on the pavement perked up fast upon seeing me. 'Raven! Raven!' they started to shout. 'Over here!'

I ran down the street as fast as my red soles would carry me so the paps' first few frames could have only been of my retreating back (and *that* bag). Doing a sneaky sidestep in those damn tiny stilettos, I was fast leaving the flashbulb frenzy in my wake when

I realised the major flaw in my hasty plan: how the hell was I supposed to get out of there?

I looked around desperately, my vision not aided any by the fact I was wearing plastic sunglasses in the dark.

Suddenly, a drunken woman stopped me in my tracks. 'Oh my god! Raven! Can I *please* get a picture?' she screeched.

I agreed to the star shot while frantically looking for an exit, a fatal pause that gave the snappers enough time to catch up.

'Raven! Oi, Raven!' they vied for my attention. The paps and my fan snapped away blithely as I stood frozen to the spot.

Shit.

Out of the corner of one UV-protected eye, I spotted an idling taxi. Rescue! I headed for it immediately, blisters forming on my feet as I ran.

As I opened the back door, the photogs were still calling Raven's name, so I waved before jumping into the revving vehicle and burying my face in my hands.

The cabbie didn't need an explanation. Although he'd probably never heard of Raven, he sped us away from the pap pack. Once we were safely away from the club, I took off the sunnies and tied my hair back, instantly de-Ravenising myself.

'Can you please go around the block a few times and then head back to the club?' I requested, crossing my fingers that my hostage hadn't high-tailed it in the meantime.

As I had hoped, the photographers had dispersed as soon as they got their shot, so after a few laps in the taxi the coast was clear enough for me to venture inside to retrieve Raven. Slipping the driver a wad of notes to sit and wait out the front, I clattered inside Kit and Kaboodle for the second time that morning.

Racing up the stairs and into the toilets, I tried to bury the awful scenarios that were racing through my head. What if Raven wasn't there? What if Raven was there but in a coke-induced coma? What if Raven was there and was wondering why her publicist had cruelly stripped her down, stolen her clothes and left her locked in a dingy toilet?

I needn't have worried.

'Did you find any coke?' was her first question as I pushed open the cubicle door. Her pupils were the size of serving platters and the occasional droplet of blood from her nose stained Teri Hatcher's face on my T-shirt.

Relieved, I dragged Raven to her feet and bundled her out into the early morning air. Around us, addicts slumped in back lanes, while the young and the beautiful emerged from night-clubs all along the street. Raven, sans shoes, and me, sans sleep, fitted in perfectly. Never mind Wisteria Lane, this was one crazy neighbourhood.

2

If ever the Sartorialist was likely to be in Sydney, today was going to be the day.

I couldn't tell you how many working hours I'd lost to planning what I'd wear the day the influential blogger popped up in the Pacific on one of his visits Down Under. (A Jil Sander maxi skirt in orange, with a tight white Bassike tee and toting a matching Chanel 2.55 was my current favourite ensemble, incidentally.) But Murphy's law said the Sartorialist was never going to be around when I was at my Jil Sander best. Oh no. Just as buttered toast that will always land face down and Joan Rivers will always land face up (all that collagen must surely make her facial features the lightest, most buoyant part of her anatomy, right?), the Sartorialist was sure to be in town on the day I looked like a train wreck.

As I sat slumped in the front seat of a taxi at 6 am, glancing furtively around for any signs of his iconic camera, I prayed today wasn't my shot at internet infamy. Not the way I looked off the back of three hours' sleep. Not having spent the remainder of my night wrestling Raven out of a cab and into her suite at the Park Hyatt, where I removed her makeup, fed her water and painkillers and put her to bed. Not when I had only a couple of hours to turn myself around and haul my arse back to the office to face Diane. I tried to push all thoughts of the Sartorialist out of my mind because, with my luck, just thinking about the style-savvy snapper would be enough to conjure him up.

As we pulled up in my driveway that morning, I half-leapt, half-fell out of the taxi in my rush to get inside. Going to pay, I fumbled through my bag for my wallet and found . . . nothing. What the fuck? Smiling apologetically at the cabbie I sat back down on the front seat to rummage properly. Makeup bag? Check. BlackBerry? Check. Business cards, Raven's publicity schedule, spare business cards? Check, check, check. 'I know my wallet's in here somewhere,' I said aloud, trying to reassure myself as much as the driver. It's not like Raven would bother pilfering from a non-celeb (or 'street person', as she preferred) like me. As my hands felt frantically around the interior of my oversized Louis Vuitton Speedy 40 I felt a slit in the iconic brown lining and my hand wrapped around my wallet. Perf! Cursing ole Louie for his intricate design work, I reefed my wallet out of my bag and slipped the cabbie his fare. And then some. 'Sorry, bud,' I said and finally headed for my front door.

Once inside, I made a beeline for the bathroom and a steaming hot shower. No time later I was schlepping through Paddo with my laptop, pausing only to inhale a skim mocha. Takeaway coffee was an indulgence in which I rarely partook, preferring to put my spare change towards the eBay piggy bank, but sleepless nights chaperoning cokehead celebs was a sound excuse to splurge. Taking a swig of my mocha, I threw five Nurofen tablets down my throat for good measure. I know, I know, Nurofen tablets, like designer shoes, are generally best when they come in pairs. Not in odd numbers and certainly not in clusters of five. But, again not unlike designer shoes, I found the effect the pain-relief medication had on my mental state was both soothing and uplifting. Serenity in a tab, if you will. Even if there was no actual chemical reason for it, a small handful of Nurofen could calm my nerves and allay all tension much more effectively than booze or illegal pills could ever hope to do. Plus, of course, Nurofen wielded the added bonus of being a hell of a lot cheaper than the aforementioned designer shoes. And so I scoffed them regularly and excessively and had been doing so for four years now, the exact same four years that I had been working at Wilderstein PR. A fact that was no mere coincidence.

At the thought of my employer, those butterflies took up residence in my stomach again. As I waited for my Nurofen panacea to kick in I contemplated what lay in wait for me at the office. Had I pulled it off? What was Diane going to say? Would everyone believe it was Raven in the photos?

Thankfully, Oxford Street in the morning is always a welcome distraction and today proved no exception. Heading towards the imaginary but all-important barrier between Paddington and Darlinghurst I watched the prostitutes call it a night and hobble home, the bottoms of their acrylic heels worn down to a nub of plastic the size of a twenty cent piece. A man walked past talking violently to himself; two guys in tight white singlets skipped down the footpath singing Kylie Minogue songs to one another. There were still people stumbling out of bars, with loosened ties and beer-stained shirts, making me feel marginally better about my own sorry state.

Better, that is, until I reached Wilderstein PR.

As I stared up at the imposing building before me, all metal and glass and as shiny and severe as Anna Wintour's signature bob, I felt my stomach sink. Despite having worked there for almost four years, I would never get used to running the gauntlet of the Wilderstein wilderness each morning. It was a jungle in there. A jungle where every elevator stop and every encounter in the foyer was just another opportunity to be eaten alive.

At the top of the food chain are the Wives. So called (in my mind, at least) because the treatment I receive from these women each day is not unlike the response you might expect if you'd just strolled into work having slept with each of their husbands. Repeatedly. And enjoyed it. The Wives are kings of the jungle here and you fuck with them at your peril. In fact, if David Attenborough ever got bored of stalking the savannas of the Serengeti and instead stumbled into the microcosm of Wilderstein PR, he'd probably classify the Wives thus: 'As easily identified by the lavish designer handbags worn on their bony arms as by the ice-cold stares on their frozen faces, these women are the undisputed matriarchs of the industry. With BlackBerrys surgically attached to the sides of their heads and their bodies covered with distinctive luxury labels, these creatures habitually refuse to remove their sunglasses before midday. And only ever after imbibing an espresso or two.'

And while the Wives don't like to get their manicured hands dirty with the day-to-day drudgery of publicity schedules, these women run the business and provide the (very Botoxed) public faces of their company's campaigns: schmoozing clients, pampering the press and lunching like it's 1985.

As for their prey? When not dining with potential clients, the Wives generally feast on the less experienced in the industry: the Young Wives. The Young Wives are power-hungry wannabes and are easily identified in the wild as they dress almost exclusively in fashion-slave black, as if headed to the older Wives' funerals. Mostly made up of publicists and senior publicists, the Young Wives are partial to fronting up for work dripping in accessories in an attempt to make them appear larger and more threatening to the predatory Wives. As if trying to differentiate themselves from the older species, the Young Wives say things like 'totes' and 'cute', yet just like the more powerful predators, their facial movements never match their words.

Then, of course, there are the Teenage Brides. These junior publicists and admin assistants are best known for parading in the office environ looking like they're off for a day at the races. Clad in skin-tight dresses, short skirts, pink lipstick and the odd fascinator or beret, the Teenage Brides make for easy prey.

So that's who's who in the zoo. Of course, when it comes to PR – Public Relations, Press Reps, Promo & Rumour, whatever you want to call it – we're all fighting for the same space on the same social pages and in the same gossip columns of the very same newspapers. Not to mention the fact each and every one of us is trying to nab each other's clients in order to climb the slippery rungs of the PR career ladder. In the dog-eat-dog world of publicity, it really was a wonder I got out of Wilderstein alive each day.

There was only one thing Diane hated more than failing to achieve quality media coverage for a client, and that was losing her luggage.

Me? I could think of at least half a dozen worse fates that might befall a person in the name of work. Losing a night's sleep babysitting a cokehead celeb in the Cross. Or losing your dignity impersonating said celeb. Even losing the will to live when your boss found out. But losing your luggage? Not even in my top ten.

Diane, however, was neurotic about it. So much so that she refused to take any luggage on her flights and instead had all her belongings couriered between destinations when travelling. Regardless of location. Just one month into my job my sweaty palms had had to sign for a $987.35 express delivery from Diane's summer holiday in Spain (complete with duty-free cigarette and alcohol purchases). A fee Diane hadn't batted a Botoxed eyelid over. In fact, Diane habitually had her bags picked up the night before she boarded a flight, ensuring nothing but a Louis Vuitton carry-on and her handbag (the label of which depended on the day; given today was Thursday, my money was on her large quilted aged-calfskin Chanel tote, from the Paris-Byzance collection) was at the mercy of our international airline services.

So it was no surprise, then, to see a FedEx courier turn up at the frosted-glass double doors of the office shortly after I arrived at work. Even before I signed the release I knew what the delivery was. Diane's luggage from Melbourne. Of course, whichever minion accepted the delivery was duly obliged to go through the luggage and send certain items off to the drycleaners. However, contain your excitement. This wasn't nearly as voyeuristic as it sounds. Not risking our grubby fingers fondling her fashion valuables, Diane put everything in specially ordered vacuum-sealed bags labelled CLEAN, KEEP AWAY and NEVER! I'd only once peeked inside NEVER! and had been disappointed to discover the Pandora's box of Diane's luggage simply held a selection of not-yet-released age-resistant face creams. Creams I hopefully didn't yet need and would NEVER! be able to afford anyway.

Deciding to dump Diane's laundry on my way to the Look shoot with Raven, I left her luggage to one side and turned my attention to my emails. Only one hundred odd since last night. Fantastic. I scanned through them and pulled out the relevant ones.

From: Caroline Monae
Title: Stylist, Look magazine
Time: 07.52 am

Hey Jasmine. All prepped for today's shoot. Clothes have arrived, all in 'rock chic' as requested and we also received the underwear you sent over. Just confirming Raven will be on site at 9 am. And will she need anything else?

Reply: Caroline, hi. All good for today. Should be on time. Yes there are extra requirements, unfortunately. My apologies. Double the water, triple the Berocca and can we please have some vodka on standby just in case? We all know the transformative power of hair of the dog, right? Most importantly, I need to collect all confidentiality agreements from staff before we start, please. See you soon!

From: Will
Title: Boyfriend
Time: 8.07 am

Hey babe. Just got up and saw your text. Why you up so early? Let me guess — at the office already? Wanna grab a quick bite tonight before you start at the bar? Italian? Xxxxxx

Reply: OMG. Long story. Text you later OK? Mwa xxxxxx

From: Harry Serino
Title: Client—Managing Director for Converse
Time: 07.01 am

Morning! Received the images from last week's shoot but they are only hard copies. Is that strange? Can you please call the photographer, get the disk, talk them through with Diane and get back to me ASAP. We know which ones we like and are keen to see if you pick the same. I have total faith in you, kiddo. HS

Reply: *All over it, Haz. Just quietly, I don't really trust your creative opinion. Kidding! Will come back to you in no time. JL*
PS *How did Lisa go with finding a dress? And stop calling me kiddo!*

From: Marlita Nikolovski
Title: Talent manager, Raven
Time: 08.09 am

Have just arrived at Raven's room and she has not had a good night's sleep. In fact, she's feeling awful. Any chance of moving the shoot?

Reply: Unfortunately, Marlita, it is impossible to move the shoot. Look is paying for this time and they're on deadline and going to print this afternoon. I have a limo waiting downstairs for you two and there is a team of people ready to make Raven look a million bucks. Please tell her everything will be fine and she still has this afternoon off.

    Call me with any problems.

From: Peter Middleton
Title: Director of Communications, Havu Island Bali
Time: 04.23 am

Elle McFearsome has arrived! V exciting! V diva! Call for details.

Reply: Fantastic. A certain reporter is gagging for the goss. Will call lunchtime your time, J

My sortie into the scintillating world of Outlook was interrupted by a text from Diane. My butterflies flooded back with force.

I trust you worked out last night's situation. Have just landed. Car better be ready.

Shit! I hadn't triple-checked the hire car. Or checked at all! Gah! I madly dialled Sam's number. A number, sadly, I know by heart.

'Hello, Mizz Lewis,' he answered on the second ring.

'Hello, Sam. Please tell me you're at the airport?'

'It's your lucky day, Jazzy baby. I am outside the closest exit to her gate right now.'

'Are her cigarettes at the ready?'

'Of course. Waiting on the seat with an ashtray I polished personally before leaving HQ.'

'And her short black?'

'Done. Sans lid, naturally.'

Bless this man.

'Once again, Sam, you're the man of my dreams. Can you please tell her from me that everything is fine and both the client and I are en route to our appointment?'

'Will do.'

'Love your work. Have a great day!'

My butterflies stopped their fluttering. But only for a minute. Realising the time, I launched myself from my desk, Diane's dirty laundry in my arms. Pausing for a micro second by Anya's desk, I asked if she wanted to come along with me to the *Look* shoot. Safety in numbers and all that. She didn't need a second invitation. To Anya, celeb status was worth more than a final season McQueen. She collected famous encounters like other people collect *Muse* magazine. It was as if she harboured some bizarre notion that 'celebrity' might one day rub off on her if only she could rub up against enough stars. I, on the other hand, preferred to think of fame as a sexually transmitted disease. It didn't matter how many vaccinations they introduced for teenage girls, when it came to celebrities: vote one abstinence, I said.

3

Several years back, over two hundred and fifty stiletto-loving Sydneysiders put their best three-inch-heel-clad foot forward and ploughed up an eighty-metre race track at Sydney's Circular Quay, breaking the world record for the most people running in a 'stiletto sprint'. While I didn't lace up my Louboutins and join them, if ever they repeated the stunt I was in serious shape to take out line honours given the speed at which I ran – in heels – into the drycleaners to drop off Diane's laundry that day. And then I was back in the taxi faster than you could say 'blisters'.

'Okay, the Ivy on George Street, please,' Anya said to the cab driver as I rubbed my aching ankles.

Look had chosen the Ivy Penthouse as the shoot location because it was decadent, a little retro and spacious enough to transform into anything you needed. Plus, as this was an underwear shoot, a bed was essential. Look's emphasis on top-shelf products made them the perfect fit for our market. A glossy tabloid would have only cheapened the lingerie range, and by giving Look an exclusive shoot with Raven, we were on good ground to get the cover. An international celeb with a local angle in a mag focused near-exclusively on international fashion was an ideal situation.

Opening the door to the Penthouse, we were greeted by three bulging racks of designer clothing. By the tranquillity of the room I knew Raven hadn't yet arrived. After introductions with the stylist, her assistants, the fashion editor and some runners, I left Anya fawning over clothes that were to be touched (touched!) by Raven and called Marlita, Raven's manager, to check our model was still on track (and not just crack).

'We're almost there, but Raven and I have just discussed this and we would like to cut the shoot time from four to two hours because Raven is unprecedentedly jet-lagged today and really needs to rest. Thanks!' Then Marlita hung up.

A response from me was clearly not required.

Knowing full well that 'jet-lagged' means 'big night out' on a normal day, let alone one into which I had serious insight, I quietly began to panic. Raven's pill-popping excursion to Kings Cross might yet cost us the cover of Look. Not to mention my job once Diane found out.

You see, while Marlita, as Raven's manager, was technically responsible for making sure the talent didn't go off the rails, my role as publicist had the dubious distinction of having no clear distinction. As long as the client was happy, the talent was happy and Diane was not homicidal, I could rest easy. Easy, huh? In short, when Raven was in town and spruiking our client's products, it was my job to make sure all headlines were good headlines. Whatever that might take.

A text came through from Zoe, another of the senior publicists at Wilderstein: *So Raven is headline news. Only the article fails to mention why she is here in Australia. Is this your fuck-up? Why was Raven even out in the Cross?* Zoe attached a link to a US gossip site that I promptly pasted into the browser on my BlackBerry. The headline read: CAN'T KEEP *AWAY* FROM THE CLUBS BUT SEEMINGLY SOBER: RAVEN REMAINS A GOOD GIRL DOWN UNDER.

I waited anxiously for the photo to load. It's hard to describe the feeling of seeing a picture of yourself, one that is captioned as someone famous, on an American gossip website that is read by millions of people a day. I couldn't stop staring at it and, with my eyes still glued to the screen, I raced straight out to the balcony to read the story.

Reformed LA party princess Raven was spotted leaving an Australian nightclub earlier this morning. But don't worry, the one-time off-the-rails singer has not returned to her bad-girl ways. Witnesses report the YouTube phenomenon was calm and collected when she left Sydney hotspot Kit and Kaboodle, despite the local time being 4 am!

The photographer who took these photos said Raven kindly posed for pictures with a fan while smiling and waving for their own shots. Quite a world away from her regular behaviour, wouldn't you agree? Unaided by any handlers, Raven even took a cab by herself back to the hotel, which is unheard of for a celeb visiting another country. Good to see you've got your feet planted firmly on Aussie soil, Raven.

Wow. I did it! This was beyond! Aside from the fact the gossip site believed the person in the picture was Raven, Zoe was none the wiser and she sat next to me every day at work! Thank. God.

Of course, our client hadn't been mentioned, which Diane was not going to be happy about. But it was a helluva lot better than any kind of 'Raven Goes Wild Again' story, which would have dragged the name of our client's underwear range through the mud. And then some.

Anya spotted my celebration dance on the balcony and could tell there was more going on than just a retweet of one of my clients' products. She wandered over to see. I simply held my phone out for her to read the article.

'Gah! There's not a single mention of Vixenary in that piece! Why are you smiling? Are you on crack?'

I danced some more. 'Can you tell it's not Raven in that article but just a good lookalike?' I asked.

'Nooo,' Anya said incredulously. 'Who is it?'

I stabbed my finger into my chest then held it up to my lips to indicate she should keep that quiet.

'Holy shit!' she whispered. 'That's you?'

I nodded proudly.

'I can't believe you passed for a celeb, babe!'

38

Typical Anya. She was more impressed by my brush with stardom than my brush with unemployment. I started smiling again but caught a glimpse of myself in one of the full-length mirrors that adorned the walls of the living room and realised I was still in a bad way. Raven, the skank, was cutting the shoot in half and Diane still hadn't called. Usually I couldn't escape her. I frowned and the creases on my skin looked ten times worse underneath the heavy foundation I had lacquered on earlier. However, like the strange gratification one gets from seeing Oxford Street revellers of a morning, once Raven actually arrived, I felt instantly better.

She looked like total shit. Even in sunglasses.

It was as if she hadn't bothered to shower and had decided to hang on to the tow bar of the limo and be dragged through the city. The crown of her hair was stuck to her scalp, and was that cigarette ash I could see in there? Even Anya struggled to look impressed.

Caz, the stylist, mouthed the magic word, 'Airbrushing,' before smiling and looking at Raven, who walked straight to the cans of Red Bull arrayed on of the catering table, her head down, her manager following, still on the phone.

With the Look team standing around awkwardly, and Anya frozen like a deer in the headlights of fame, I decided to approach.

'Morning, Raven. How are we feeling today? And how great is this location?' I tried, smiling ferociously and waiting for the recognition to kick in.

She stared at me blankly, her bottom lip so dry that it looked like it was about to snap off. 'Who are you?' she groaned.

'I'm Jasmine, the publicist who has been looking after you all week,' I said sweetly. 'I saw you last night?' I added, tilting my head meaningfully at her.

'Riiiiiiight. So I guess you're the one who can explain why the fuck there are photos circling the fucking USA of me in dirty piece-of-shit sunglasses,' she said.

'Sorry?' I replied, still smiling sweetly, when I remembered the knock-off D&Gs I had paid stupid money for. And I believe she meant 'circulating' rather than 'circling'.

'Are you deaf? There are fucking pictures of me from last night in these fucking fake Dolces and all my friends have texted me saying how fucking cheap I look. I mean . . . what the farrrk,' she said. 'As if I would ever wear those. What the farrrk?'

I stood by silently, not quite believing what was happening. Sure, I didn't expect her to name her firstborn in my honour, but a little gratitude would have been nice.

'Raven, let's get on with this,' said Marlita, finally off the phone.

'Fine. But I'm leaving in, like, two hours, no later, and there better be some good food. Faark this shit,' she said, no doubt still under the influence.

I glanced at the *Look* staffers. They just looked petrified.

'Okay then.' I clapped. 'Raven, if you'd like to come with me and one of the runners, we'll show you to the bathroom. The facilities here are five-star and will have everything you need. Once you're showered, hair and makeup will be waiting,' I said, winking at hair and makeup, who nodded in nervous agreement.

Raven just shrugged and puffed her lips into a very unattractive pout.

Guiding her to the shower I began to form a PR plan in my mind. I ran back through the penthouse bedroom to the lounge where everyone was assembled and went over to where the Look girls and Anya were huddled. I assured them the shoot was going to last the full four hours and, although Raven was undoubtedly going to be difficult, there would be an added bonus: an interview – 'Raven's fashion dos and don'ts'. This was not part of the original contract so was met with surprised enthusiasm. Especially from Anya. It was like telling them a dress they had initially assumed was from Katies was actually Roland Mouret.

Now for the second part of the plan. Stalking over to Marlita I told her I had a solution to the bad press Raven was receiving at home because of those *awful* sunnies. 'Who knows where on earth she got them. It's a disaster,' I added, throwing my hands about for emphasis. 'Now, if Raven will agree to submit an interview to Look right now on fashion mishaps, like "Not borrowing your friend's sunglasses" for instance, I can ensure the story is syndicated to the States. The problem will be cleared up before she even arrives home. Of course, if Raven is too jet-lagged to conduct the interview herself Wilderstein PR can come up with the quotes and send them through to you for copy approval . . .'

Marlita tapped her phone against her chin for a moment before agreeing. 'Although I don't want to bother Raven with an interview. Let's work on it together, shall we?' she said, an eyebrow raised.

'Perfect,' I replied just as Raven reappeared in a fluffy white robe. She snatched a bottle of Santa Vittoria water from Anya, who was hovering near the action, and I actually thought Anya might faint from the close encounter.

For a day that had started so awfully (and so damned long ago), things were starting to look up. And then my phone vibrated. A text from Diane and the first contact I'd had with her since early this morning: *My office. As soon as the shoot is finished. Do you understand?* Oh, I understood . . .

4

'OMG. Why on earth would you allow her to be seen in public with those *disgusting* sunglasses?' Diane fumed, her own sunglasses still covering her eyes, the Dior insignia glistening in the early afternoon sun that streamed into her office.

'Diane, it was actually —'

'And why, *why* would you allow those photographers — four photographers, I'm told on good authority — to snap the talent and leave without so much as a pair of Vixenary knickers? Our client who has *paid for our representation!*' Behind her sunnies her eyes flashed and I was reminded of a bull preparing to charge.

'Diane, I'm sorry, I —'

'Jasmine, don't you understand,' her voice rose in fury, 'that I was on an interstate visit trying to consolidate a deal? A deal that will blow the roof off every other office in this building! Don't you?' She circled, enraged. If this was going to be a bullfight I was preparing to be gored.

'I do, I just —'

'And do you not realise that I have to go away on these trips, and I need to be able to trust my employees to take care of everything when I do?'

'Completely. And I was doing that when —'

'Then, Jasmine, why are there photos of Raven on the home page of every gossip site in the United States of America without so much as a mention of our client in the goddamn caption?'

There was nothing for it but to wave the proverbial red rag. 'It's not Raven in the picture, it's me!' I blurted.

Silence.

God, someone pass me a sangria.

Diane looked at me through her black tinted sunnies before slowly sitting down at her desk. Removing her glasses with painstaking care, she studied her computer screen for a moment. 'Hmm,' she conceded. 'It is you. You do look remarkably like her. I never would have guessed. Quite a master of disguise, aren't you?' she added, staring at me intently.

I shuffled uncomfortably under her gaze, not convinced she wasn't coming back for round two. 'Er, not really. I just did what I had to do. Raven was too wasted to run the pap gauntlet so I did it for her. When the paparazzi left, I doubled back and took Raven home to her hotel. That's why I couldn't talk to the photogs about the client. I am sorry about that,' I said, feeling no remorse whatsoever at having disappointed Diane. And especially not given the way she was wiping the floor with me now. What I *was* sorry about was having missed an opportunity for publicity for my client. Something I never liked to do.

'Well,' she said dismissively, 'it still doesn't solve what I'm going to tell my client now, does it?'

'But have you seen the *Sun*'s story about Raven this morning?' I asked.

On my way home from today's shoot I'd had the foresight to call Luke Jefferson, gossip columnist for the *Sun* newspaper, and fill him in about what had happened last night in the Cross. By offering him more details than had been reported in the USA, including details of the labels 'Raven' was wearing, I'd managed to convince him to run the story with a plug for Vixenary included. Predictably, Diane had been out having a smoke on her balcony when I returned to the office, so I'd had about a three-second window to check the story was up online and to save my arse. It was and I had.

'I see,' was Diane's only response after sighting the piece. She reached instinctively for a cigarette. 'You'll have to send the web link to the client.'

'Done. Just now. They should have already seen it, in fact. I can let you know when they respond, if you like?'

'Hmm. Please do. Back to it now.'

And with that, cigarette in one hand and Diors in the other, Diane headed out to her balcony.

Olé.

Back at my desk, I started ploughing through my emails. Later that evening, of course, I had to work at Mrs Sippy in Paddington where Diane was hosting some product launch. Manning the door at Wilderstein PR events was required as part of my contract with Diane (and also by my rent-hungry real estate agent). PR might not pay so well but it expects a helluva lot, and standing around all night outside Mrs Sippy was considered just one more facet of my day job.

But being a door bitch is not the only way PR sucks you dry. Like, I earn about thirty thousand dollars a year before tax yet I'm still supposed to be in possession of the finest quality products, products on par with the celebrities and clients I'm representing. Because no star, journo or agent is going to believe you know what you're talking about in this industry if you turn up to a media call dressed in clothes from MINKPINK and with jewellery by Diva. No way.

As I regrouped in front of my computer screen, Anya sauntered by my desk looking like the cat that had got the McQueen.

'Why so chuffed, babe?' I asked.

'Boom!' was Anya's response, as she threw a small zip-lock bag onto my keyboard.

The bag was stuffed with red silky material and was labelled in handwritten black marker: *Vixenary, Sabotage collection, worn by Raven for Look on . . .*

'OMFG!' I yelped. 'Are you mad? Why the fuck do you have Raven's dirty knickers?'

Anya looked hurt. 'Don't you know anything about celebrity memorabilia, dude? I'm going to retire to the Bahamas on the money I make from that g-string one day. Just think what you could get for one of Madonna's bras now.'

Somehow I didn't think Raven's filthy laundry ranked up there with Madge's iconic Gaultier brassiere, but I didn't say that to Anya, who was clearly off the air on this one.

'How did you even get this?' I asked.

'Oh, easy,' Anya said. 'Raven just dumped every item she modelled this morning straight on the floor after she'd worn it. I could take my pick.'

This was true, I'd seen her in action. The diva had unceremoniously dropped all of Vixenary's new range on the floor, like a petulant teenager, as soon as each shot had been taken by the *Look* photog. The kid was not at all fazed by stripping off in front of a roomful of strangers.

But the fact her knickers had only been worn for two minutes did not mean it wasn't beyond revolting that they were now Glad-bag fresh and lying on my desk.

'How do you even plan to –' I began, when suddenly Diane materialised among the plebs and started heading for my desk. This could not be good. Diane never left the sanctuary of her lavish office for the sweatshop of our cubicles.

Anya vanished, sans smalls. Having a minor heart attack, I flicked Raven's g off my keyboard with a ruler and it landed in my gaping LV handbag lying under my desk. Diabolical! I'd have to deal with that later.

'Jasmine!' shrieked Diane. She hadn't seen the knickers, had she? I couldn't be sure I'd moved fast enough to escape her eagle eyes. 'Where is my blue Issa dress?' she demanded.

Her blue Issa dress? Was this a trick question? That particular number was currently sitting in a pile of dirty laundry at the drycleaners where I'd dumped it this morning.

'Er, it's at the drycleaners just like you asked,' I stammered.

'Well, I want it for tonight's launch at Icebergs,' came the reply as she stalked off. No discussion to be entered into.

Great. How was I supposed to perform that small miracle? I wondered as I reached for my phone to dial the poor drycleaners, Raven's knickers temporarily forgotten.

Would this day never end?

Coming home from work that evening, I made a long-overdue call to my boyfriend, Will. A long-overdue phone call to my long-past-his-used-by-date boyfriend, I should say. You see, Will and I had an enduring relationship, but only enduring because he hadn't had the balls, or I the time away from work, for either of us to terminate it yet. Let me explain.

Will Jamieson and I began our relationship at work. And things went downhill from there. As a one-time client of Wilderstein PR, Will used to swan into our offices for his weekly campaign meeting doused in so much aftershave you could smell him coming even before the lift doors had opened. The guy flirted with the receptionist and winked at the junior account managers, before plonking himself down on the nearest ergonomic chair and sliding around the office floor making a menace of himself and a headache for me. Will Jamieson spoke too slow and moved too fast; he was careless and cocky and work-shy and arrogant. But he was persistent. And so I fell for him eventually.

Now, several years later, all the foibles that had initially bugged me about Will were still there. It was just that now he'd had time to discover a few of mine too. Like spending too much money on shoes and too little time in his company and, worst of all in his eyes, too much of my life in the office. Consequently, our relationship was a tempestuous one. Will and I fell out loudly and we fell out often, and then he would pack whatever of his worldly wares were lying around my flat into a garbage bag, sling it over his shoulder and swear that he would never return and that we were over. Of course, he always did and we never were. But it was only a matter of time.

'Sorry, babe,' I began my now-familiar spiel on the phone to Will. 'I would have called sooner but you wouldn't believe what an awful day this has been.'

'That's cool. Is everything okay?'

'Yeah, it's fine now,' I assured him, glossing over my 3 am wake-up call, my impersonation of a Hollywood celebrity and my encounter with Diane in the office, not to mention my emergency dash to the drycleaners where, through a combination of sweet-talking and an even sweeter tip, I'd managed to rescue one royal-blue dress for Her Highness. 'My day is one long story and I can't afford the phone bill so I'll fill you in when I see you next.'

'You could tell me tonight when I take you to dinner. How about that?'

'Sorry?' I replied distractedly as I searched through my bag for the client briefing notes I'd brought with me as homework.

'Dinner? Tonight? You and me?' Will tried again.

'Okay, so here's another apology,' I said. 'I have to go see Shelley tonight before work at Mrs Sippy. I'm really sorry. I would have loved to catch up with you but I haven't seen Shell in forever.'

There was silence on the line for a moment.

'And I've started to forget what my girlfriend looks like so I kinda wanted to see her.'

I tried to keep my sigh inaudible as I began scanning the briefing notes while I talked. 'Well, I'm about five foot six, blonde hair, hazel eyes and I miss you terribly.'

'Yeah, yeah. But Shelley's wardrobe is more important than me, right?'

'No,' I assured him lamely. 'Well, not unless she's acquired a new lime Birkin since I was last there.'

My attempt at humour fell flat.

'Fine. Whatever.'

Will hung up and I continued teetering down Oxford Street, parting post-work pedestrians and pretending to care about our aborted phone call. The Shelley I was heading for was Shelley Shapiro, my oldest friend and sartorial saviour. Shelley and I met when we attended the same private girls high school and she was bullying the other kids with her quick wit and fearless attitude. We clicked immediately. Sadly, Shelley's dad wasn't in the picture and her mum passed away just before her eighteenth birthday, leaving Shelley with an empty home but a very full trust fund. No matter how much money Shell burned through, she would never be anything but beyond comfortable. Now, financial, footloose and fancy free, she viewed herself as a full-time fashionista. Her raison d'être was shopping. And Shell was staunchly a 'one-wear' only girl, so her hand-me-downs were legendary. Well, this plus the fact Shelley suffered from an unfortunate case of body dysmorphia. A gorgeous and curvy size four, Shelley was convinced she was a size zero. Consequently, she spent a fortune on the latest designer clothes, in the smallest available sizes, only to then gift them to me.

Turning into Shelley's driveway in Woollahra was like visiting Gatsby's humble abode. Her recycling bin stood sentry out the front, stuffed full of iconic black Net-a-Porter delivery boxes and the odd empty bottle of Moët. Her sleek grey Porsche sat in the drive, the keys dangling temptingly in the ignition.

I waltzed through her open front door, my laptop bag banging against the intercom. 'Shell?' I bellowed down the marble hallway.

'Sweetie!' A figure clad in white emerged at the end of the hall, holding two glasses in front of her. 'I was just about to call you! The wine is getting warm and we can't have that!'

Shelley tottered down the corridor then stopped dead. 'Oh my god,' she said, lowering the glasses to chest level. 'You look like shit!'

'Thanks, hon.'

'Seriously, you do. What's wrong? Is it Will?'

'No, just work as ever.' I grabbed the glass that wasn't covered in lipstick. 'And it's not over yet. Tonight I have the very great pleasure of standing outside a club for five hours. FAB!'

We clinked glasses and plonked ourselves down on her Missoni-covered bar stools.

'Dah-ling, I don't know why you are still carrying on as a bloody door bitch,' Shelley said, swigging her sav blanc.

'Shell, you know I have to. Girl's gotta pay the rent, right?'

'Oh babe, fair enough,' she said sympathetically. 'And, while it won't pay the rent, I do have something that might make up for the fact you flog yourself senseless every day.'

Running upstairs – no mean feat after her three glasses of vino to my three sips – Shelley was back down the impressive spiral in no time with a hessian bag promisingly labelled *Balmain*.

'Here,' she said, thrusting it at me. 'I don't want it any more. I think my initial love for it was merely a projection of knowing you would adore it, you know? I haven't even worn it. Just not my style, really.'

I looked at her like a kid scoring a bat mitzvah gift, then opened the bag and pulled out a magnificent wide-shouldered black jacket decorated with studs placed randomly down the collar.

'Oh. My. God,' was all I could manage as I put it against my body.

'Divine, right? It's only just hit the stores.' Shelley winked.

Decadent tails sat tightly on the waistline, hugging the stomach, while the shoulder pads trapezed out ever so flatteringly beyond the arms.

'Shell, I couldn't possibly take this. The tag is still on! You could totally take it back.'

'Oh babe, that's never going to happen.'

'Honestly, Shell, borrowing something like this is just as special as owning it.'

'Dah-ling, you know I'd never let you hire out an item. I want you to bond with this Balmain. Develop a deep and meaningful relationship with this Balmain. Don't wear it and return it like some desperado celebrity coat hanger, snapped once in lay-by couture in a vain attempt to resurrect their profile.'

I laughed. 'Like the wardrobe equivalent of *Dancing with the Stars*?'

'Exactly! Or the sartorial substitute for a sex tape! Now,' Shelley went on, 'in return for the new addition to your wardrobe, I've got a teeny favour to ask: can you sort out mine?' She gestured towards the dining room table, which was littered with shopping bags and clothes still on hangers.

I shook my head in wonderment at what was coming.

'Any chance you could pop these things onto eBay for me?' Shelley asked. 'They're all *so* over, it's just not funny.'

'Sweetie, you know I will. Or I can show you how to do it yourself and you could make a small fortune without having to get up off the couch. It's really easy.' It wasn't that I minded selling Shelley's stuff online for her and then popping her profits into her bank account so she could spend them all over again, it was just that I couldn't quite grasp the invisible but all-important line Shelley had drawn between selling her own clothes on eBay and having me do it for her.

'Oh, never!' Shelley said, mortified. 'I could never stoop so low as to use that lazy woman's approach to shopping. No offence.'

'None taken,' I said, giving up yet again on her logic and going back to admiring the Balmain beauty.

'The point of shopping is to actually go into a bloody shop!' she continued. 'Browsing, trying on the same thing in three different sizes, asking the staff for a discount. It's a whole package, not just using a mouse and typing in your credit card details. That is just plain lazy.'

'And yet you're more than happy to have people buy your things online,' I smirked. I couldn't resist.

'Ugh. I am merely manipulating the pathetic so-called "consumers" who can't be bothered leaving their homes. Hopefully one day they will realise they have been ripped off and will actually enter a store every now and then.'

'If it means my label lifeline runs out, I sincerely hope not!'

'Stick with me, sweets. You'll be fine.'

'You're sure I can have this?' I held up the Balmain jacket and checked one last time.

'Dah-ling. Celebrities can borrow. My sister can borrow. Magazines can borrow. You deserve to own. And you need it! Good clothes are a PR staple!'

Now, how could I argue with that?

5

If you believe our press, life in Sydney is all about sex and sunshine and sinking your toes in the sand on Bondi Beach. Maybe running into Alf Stewart at the surf club. In reality, unless you're a British backpacker your day-to-day involves none of those things. In fact, with one of the longest working weeks of any country in the OECD, life as a Sydneysider is more likely to be consumed by hard slog at the office. Followed by Friday nights downing overpriced booze in an achingly hip wine bar while you talk about real estate you can't hope to afford.

The never-ending working week certainly rang true for me as I manned the door at Mrs Sippy that night in my Balmain jacket. I was doing my best to channel Abbey-Lee Kershaw on the cover of *Muse* circa '09 but feeling more like the star of one of *Wear* magazine's 'Celebs without makeup' exposés. As I shifted from one foot to the other, trying to stay awake, I contemplated what it meant to have access to all the red-carpet events and celebrities I wanted, yet to be trapped in an entry-level position. I nodded hello to the ubiquitous celebs traipsing past on their way into the launch and thought about that funny expression 'She's made it'. Most PRs in my industry would have given a year's worth of blowdries at Valonz salon to be on first-name terms with these people. And, don't get me wrong, I really liked many of them. In fact, more often than not, when I had to deal with an A-lister about product placement or a photo shoot, or even just when I ran into a 'name' at a launch party, they turned out to be lovely peeps. But let me have my Oliver Twist moment: couldn't I have some more from my career, please?

To cheer myself up, I checked my phone for tweets from Luke. As the Sun's gossip columnist, he was a very handy person for me to know. I wasn't averse to pitching story ideas to him over lunch; plus, he always had the inside on everything happening in Sydney. But our relationship meant so much more to me than just work. Luke was closer to me than most of my girlfriends, and not just because he had better dress sense than they did. (A fact that was the first thing to strike me about Luke when we met – several years ago now – at a Sydney soirée.) Of course, the second thing that struck me about Luke Jefferson that night was his dogged determination to score a scoop for his column, as he spent the entire evening coaxing and cajoling and unashamedly charming me into giving him the inside story on one of our clients and their new (and top-secret) romance. More than anyone else I've met, Luke is passionate about fashion and he's passionate about his job and, for those two reasons alone, it was (platonic) love at first sight between us. In fact, if Luke had been at all interested in skirt, and if I wasn't married to my work, ours would have been a long and beautiful relationship. As it was, it proved a pretty tight friendship.

As I leaned against the doorframe at Mrs Sippy, Luke was being as active in the social stratosphere as I'd hoped, offering Twitter fans the very latest on Belle Single's bed-hopping antics. Belle Single was an aspiring actress and the high priestess of Sydney's Sutherland Shire. More than this, though, she was a manic man-eater with a penchant for fast cars, fast men and fast-tracking her bank account.

Belle would date whoever it took in order to see her name in the headlines. I idly retweeted one of the juicier pics and Luke, who never surfaces before midday but can be relied upon at any hour of the night, responded straightaway: *@JazzyLou when can I see you for some raw slippery fish? Game on. Does Monday suit?* I texted in reply, not keen for a world's worth of Twitter stalkers to know our movements. Social columnists were God in this town and I didn't need Luke's disciples bothering us when we broke bread. *If so, midday. Done and done. Can't wait.* Lunch with Luke was exactly what I needed to get me out of my vocational funk. What I didn't need was the next text that popped up on my screen: *You missed another great night out tonight, Jazzy Lou. Your loss, not mine, Will.* Charming. I really should call him tomorrow.

By the time the little hand slipped past one, I was beyond ready to head home and reacquaint myself with my mattress. It felt like aeons since we'd last been in one another's company and we had a lot of catching up to do. I hurried back to where I'd parked my car hours earlier. Jamming the keys into the ignition I willed my old Volvo to life before easing out onto the road. My bulging LV Speedy handbag sat on the passenger seat beside me – my ideal driving companion – and I rummaged around for my lipgloss as I drove, pausing only to flick through radio stations. The dulcet tones of Richard Mercer and his ever-faithful love song dedications drifted out of the speakers and I felt a momentary pang of guilt about my own lack of dedication in that department. Little as I wanted to admit it, Will and his passive-aggressive texts had a point. I never paid Will as much attention as I awarded the rest of my life and certainly not as much as I lavished on my career. And while there was a hell of a lot that bugged me about the guy, there must have been even more that I still found attractive about him to have stuck around so long. Maybe it wasn't too late to invest a little more in our relationship.

Cruising to a halt at a lonely red light, Richard Mercer's voice pouring out of the speaker like honey, I waited sleepily for the lights to change. Then suddenly everything changed. They say in life-altering moments – those split seconds of action or inaction that you're forced to revisit for years to come – the world actually slows on its axis. It's like watching a flipped coin pivot between heads and tails in those final wobbly seconds before it falls.

As I sat at those traffic lights my passenger-side door was violently yanked open and a pale, tattooed arm reached into my car. My car. A scream rose in my throat as I slammed myself up against the driver's door, as far away from the intruder as I could get.

The lights flicked to green.

The hand was still there.

I screamed again and fumbled with my foot for the accelerator.
Fuck.

The lights glowed green, but there was no impatient CBD driver behind me to blast me with their horn. Or save me.

The hand connected with the handles of my bag and then both disappeared into the blackness.

I put my foot to the floor and screeched away from the corner, causing the passenger door to swing wildly, but I wasn't stopping for anything. I sped down the empty backstreets of Darlinghurst, the door still flapping in the breeze, my mind racing to catch up.

My bag had just been stolen.

From my car.

From inside my car.

Leaning over to slam the swinging door shut, I gave a long, guttural moan of self-pity. I had just been robbed. Oh, Shelley's beautiful bag! Oh, all my personal belongings! My BlackBerry, my laptop, my credit cards, my crappy old makeup bag. Not to mention a new box of Nurofen.

And Raven's knickers.

Shit. Anya was going to kill me. Raven's knickers were still at large somewhere in the bottom of my handbag, now itself at large in the world. This couldn't end well. At least they were freshly sealed and clearly labelled, I thought to myself, and laughed out loud at the thought. I was obviously in shock.

Dragging myself awake the next morning, my first thought was for my poor Louis Vuitton bag. Sure, it might be looking shabby and more than a little clichéd in a city where half the twenty-to thirty-year-old female demographic could be seen toting one. (Show me a private schoolgirl in Sydney who didn't receive a Speedy as their first designer bag.) But Shelley had given me that bag when I'd first started working for Diane and I'd always brandished it as a symbol of my survival. And occasionally as a shield, when Diane turned violent in the office. I knew I should have been feeling relieved I hadn't been hurt last night. And at least I still had my house keys (which had been hanging safely on my key ring in the ignition). But the hassle of reporting it to the police, filing an insurance claim and then replacing all my stuff didn't exactly fill me with joy. Not to mention surviving the next few days without my BlackBerry.

Then I remembered those damn red knickers.

How was I going to break this to Anya? I'd just destroyed her only investment plan. And probably the extent of her life savings too. Best deliver the bad news to her in person. I'd do it as soon as I got to work, I promised myself.

Then, of course, there was the risk of the press getting hold of them. After all, Raven's smalls were now in a bag with her name helpfully plastered across the front. No self-respecting journalist would require a media release urging them to turn that discovery into a headline. That's glossy-magazine heaven right there. And I'd just signed, sealed and delivered it to the world. What a helpful PR I was. Somehow I didn't think Diane would see it that way. But what could I do? Other than cross my fingers that the crim who stole my bag didn't dump it – and the knickers – somewhere the press might find it.

I hopscotched my way to work that day, more like a journo who'd lost the front page than a PR who'd misplaced some undies. Time for a quick pit stop at Oddy's Cafe for coffee? Thank you, don't mind if I do. A flying visit to Benefit to spend my only remaining cash replacing my stolen makeup essentials? *Naturellement.* Swing by the newsagent to peruse any new-release mags, you say? Why, that's practically working right there. I did manage to stop short of dropping in on Shelley for breakfast. But only just.

By the time I eventually stepped into the lift at work, I wondered what the hell was wrong with me. People in my industry got shot of their underwear in the name of career advancement on a weekly basis. This was something to put on my CV, not cause me to drag my feet all the way to the office. Admittedly it was not every day you lost *someone else's* smalls. But who was counting?

Still, by the time I got to my desk I half-expected Diane to have a warrant out with my name on it. Turns out I wasn't far wrong.

'Morning,' I said to Zoe as I plonked myself down at the desk next to hers.

'Don't talk,' she hissed, her immaculately made-up face riveted to her screen.

'Okaaay,' I said slowly, as if dragging the word out didn't count as actual speech. I'd always been unable to follow that particular instruction very well. I waited for my PC to spring to life so I could resume our conversation on email. Clearly, Diane was on the warpath.

whats the go I typed to Zoe, not bothering with the niceties of punctuation.

dunno. some sort of aggro with Vixenary, was the reply.

Fuck. The knickers.

For a moment I imagined myself and Anya trawling through some garbage-lined Darlo alleyway, sniffer dog by our side, desperately trying to track down the lowlife who had stolen my handbag so we could beg him to give us back Raven's g-string. 'Bud, g-strings are so last season.' I planned my argument in my head. 'The high-waisted brief is the item du jour, trust me. Didn't you see Bigeni's collaboration with Spanx underwear at Australian Fashion Week?'

I snapped out of it.

This was ridiculous.

There was no way in hell Vixenary even knew the red knickers were missing, let alone cared if they were. They probably gifted a thousand g-strings like that to celebs every single day. I was being paranoid.

Or not.

As I opened the first of seemingly hundreds of emails marked urgent in my inbox, my stomach sank.

From: *Anya*
Title: *Colleague*
Time: *07.58 am*

I need the knickers. Urgently.

I stood and craned my neck to see over the workstation partition. Good. Anya was still alive and kicking at her desk. You could never be sure where Diane was involved. I banged out a quick response.

> Er, teeny problem with that, love. I don't have them. I'm so, so sorry. I was robbed last night on my way home from Mrs Sippy and the knickers were in my handbag (I can explain).

The muffled sound of hope curling up its toes and dying came from Anya's direction.

Just then, Diane's door swung open seemingly unaided, as if by the sheer force of her foul temper and expensive Balenciaga perfume.

'Jasmine!' she shrilled.

Oh, God. I scuttled towards her office, bowing and scraping as I entered.

As I stood in her sprawling office suite, Diane looked me up and down, her sunglasses perched on her nose as ever. Must be concerned about her macula, I mused. She frowned as if reading my thoughts.

Don't speak until spoken to, don't speak until spoken to. My mantra played over and over in my head as I sweated it out under her glare.

'Sit,' she indicated.

I sat.

'Jasmine, perhaps you can solve a little puzzle for me?' she said.

I gulped nervously. Her Blixzed nails rapped on the desk between us.

'Perhaps you can explain to me,' she began again, 'why one of my best clients – one of this company's most lucrative and most important clients – had certain goods stolen from them?'

My eyes widened. I couldn't help it. How on earth did she know? She must have seen me flick the knickers off my desk yesterday when she came to talk about the drycleaning, and now, having not sacked any hapless member of staff lately and clearly suffering withdrawal symptoms as a consequence, she planned to exercise her HR rights on me.

We sat in silence as Diane waited for me to drop myself in it.

I scrambled to think how I could avoid dropping Anya in it.

'Ringing any bells, Jasmine?' she prodded. 'Perhaps cast your mind back to yesterday's Vixenary shoot with Raven?'

I gulped again. It was a Mexican stand-off in here but my back was flat against the wall and we both knew it.

Without warning, Anya materialised in the doorway and the world began its now all-too-familiar trick of slowing on its axis.

'It was me,' she said, falling on her sword in one fell swoop.

Diane's neck snapped around. 'What?' she demanded.

'It was me. I took the g-string from yesterday's shoot,' Anya said again. 'It was . . . it was lying on the floor and I knew Vixenary wouldn't miss it and clearly Raven didn't want it because she just left it sitting there and I'm such a big fan of Raven, oh and Vixenary too, I just love their new Sabotage range, and all I wanted was a memento of the shoot,' she raved like a dead person walking.

I couldn't sit and watch this. 'Diane, it's my fault,' I intervened. 'The underwear ended up in my bag after Anya showed it to me in the office yesterday and then my bag was stolen last night.

We'd have the knickers here now if I hadn't been robbed on my way home from Mrs Sippy.'

Diane sniffed incredulously. 'What you're saying is,' she spoke slowly, articulating every syllable, 'I'm unable to phone Vixenary and say the g-string is on its way back to them as we speak?'

Jesus Christ. As if Vixenary even knew it was missing. Moreover, why had I bothered playing the I-was-friggin'-robbed-on-the-way-home-from-slaving-my-guts-out-for-you sympathy card? Everyone knew the woman didn't have a soul.

'Yes,' I said at the same time as Anya mumbled, 'No.'

Diane got the picture. 'OMG,' she said.

I was yet to get through a meeting with Diane without at least one OMG.

'Well, pack up your desk, Anya. I won't tolerate thieving by my staff.'

Anya just nodded dumbly.

'What?' I cried. 'This is ludicrous. As if Vixenary care about a *g-string*. I bet they don't even know it's missing. And it's not Anya's fault my bag was stolen. We'd still have the stupid thing here now if it wasn't for me!'

Diane pondered this last comment as I put down the shovel from digging my own grave. Anya began sobbing quietly in the corner.

'This is ludicrous,' I repeated for good measure, although a little softer this time. 'How did you even know?'

And now Anya had been sacked. I felt awful.

Yet Diane waved away my question with a flick of her mani-cured hand, dismissing us from her office without feeling the need to explain her actions. 'Anya, security will be here in twenty minutes to escort you from the premises. Jasmine, count yourself lucky you're not going too,' was all she said.

As I comforted Anya on our dazed trek back to our desks, I pondered my so-called luck.

6

'Showwwwww me the moneyyy!' I announced, flinging a flimsy piece of paper onto the table in front of Luke as he sat sipping his Sugar Daddy cocktail in a padded booth at the Victoria Room. The British-Raj style bar was so Luke, all gilt wallpaper and slow-whirling ceiling fans. I was sure he secretly fantasised about meeting his very own Mowgli here among the jungle palms.

'I've always been more of a *Risky Business* aficionado than a *Jerry Maguire* man,' Luke said in response.

I picked up my cheque again and wafted it under Luke's nose. 'This,' I waved the cheque some more, 'is going to make me so successful that soon you'll only be able to talk to me through my publicist.'

Luke raised one eyebrow.

'Like Donald Trump says,' I went on, 'if you're going to be thinking anyway, you might as well think big.' I punctuated this with a swig of Luke's cocktail.

'That a fact, big shot?' Luke asked, sliding his drink back across the table and out of my reach. 'Well, if you plan on being that successful, you won't need a Sugar Daddy then. And how exactly, Jazzy Lou,' he went on, 'do you plan to rise up, phoenix-like, from the dust of working for Diane, huh? Tell me, I'm intrigued.'

I laughed and then paused for dramatic effect. 'I'm going to start my own business,' I said.

Silence.

'OMG, shut up!' was Luke's eventual reply.

'Totes,' I said. 'What I have in my hot little hand may look like a simple insurance cheque but this, babe, is my destiny.'

Luke rolled his eyes at my hyperbole.

I helped myself to more of his drink as I explained. 'You know how my Louis Vuitton Speedy was so cruelly ripped from my loving arms just recently? To say nothing of my BlackBerry, laptop and a small fortune in cosmetics? Well, the insurance cheque for the theft has come through and I've decided to put it towards starting my own PR company. Booom!'

Luke grinned. 'Ah-maze!' he said, stealing his glass back and raising it in a toast. 'If anyone can make it in this town, it's you, Jazzy Lou!'

Now it was my turn to grin.

'So talk me through it.' Luke retrieved the cheque that was lying between us on the table. He squinted. 'I may have failed HSC Business Studies but isn't this a little light for starting a company?'

This was true. 'Agreed. But I don't plan to go out on my own just yet. I'll invest it for a couple of years while I keep schvitzing away for Diane and learning her tricks of the trade. This is just step one in my grand master plan.'

Luke looked impressed.

'Besides,' I added, 'you're talking to the girl who currently earns less than six hundred bucks a week then dumps more than half of that into rent. I know how to make moola stretch, babe.' I took another sip of Luke's drink.

'So I see,' he said wryly. 'And you think Sydney can handle another boutique fashion PR firm? This town is looking more *Absolutely Fabulous* than a BBC remake.'

I laughed, snorting Sugar Daddy. 'Are you serious?' I said. 'Babe, over three hundred and fifty thousand Sydneysiders read the *Daily Telegraph*'s "Sydney Confidential" gossip column each day but only two hundred thousand-odd ever glance at the *Australian Financial Review*. Here, *Australia's Next Top Model* outrates the world news. Hell, there can *never* be enough fashion PRs to satiate this city.'

'Game on, then, Jazzy Lou,' said Luke.

'Game on,' I agreed. 'All I need to do is invest this baby safely for a few years while I plot my escape from Diane.'

'Speaking of, how is Cruella De Vil?' Luke asked.

I groaned and told him about poor Anya's sacking. In the weeks that had passed since she had copped the bullet, I'd done my best Florence Nightingale impersonation to nurse her back to vocational health. We'd spent several nights in retreat in her flat, updating her CV and downloading job ads. We'd cold-called and hotmailed until our little black books of industry contacts ran dry. And, while nothing had come of it yet, I knew it wouldn't be long before Anya rejoined the ranks of the PR army of Sydney. She was a gun publicist, after all. It was only when it came to celebs that her brain was shot.

Diane, meanwhile, soldiered on unscathed. It was as though the fall in employee numbers only served to boost her morale – she was never so happy as in the weeks after she'd sacked someone. Another notch in her belt, another badge on her chest. And so I avoided her like the plague. When she arrived at work each day I made sure I wasn't riding in her elevator. When she left the sanctity of her office you wouldn't see me for dust. It wasn't brave but I was no hero. My tactic of avoidance, well, it allowed me to battle on another day. I didn't plan on joining the walking wounded of Wilderstein just yet.

'Diane's a dictator!' said Luke, as if I didn't know.

'Defs,' I replied, before changing the topic. 'Now, babe, what's new with you?'

Luke grinned sheepishly. This could only mean one thing.

'No!' I cried. 'Who is he? What's his name? Where did you meet him? I can't believe you've been holding out on me the whole time I've been going on about work!'

Luke rolled his eyes. 'It would take more than a new boyfriend to distract you from work talk, Jazzy Lou.'

He had a point. 'So?' I prompted.

There was that sheepish grin again. 'So,' started Luke. 'His name's Reuben –'

'Cute,' I interrupted.

'And he lives in Double Bay and we met buying piccolo lattes at Bar Indigo and he's got the most incred collection of Italian silk bow ties, Jazzy Lou. His uncle imports them.'

I laughed at the dossier Luke presented: name, real estate, coffee preference, fashion. That's Sydney in a sentence right there.

'So when do I get to meet him?' I asked, just as my (replacement) phone vibrated on the table, announcing a text. It was Shelley: *My love, why does Marc Jacobs make everything so fucking small? Even his damn shoes don't fit! Have a pair of new season linen brogues for you. 2 die for. Swing by sometime for a pinot gris and a fitting. Mwah, Shell xxx*

I laughed and held up the screen for Luke to read.

'I see Shelley's still singlehandedly propping up the Australian economy, one size zero at a time,' Luke said, when my phone buzzed again.

This text was from Will. *Sitting at Lucios in Paddington, an open bottle of $95 chianti in front of me. On. My. Own.*

Fuck.

'Fuck!' I said, slamming my palm against my forehead. 'I'm supposed to be having dinner with Will tonight at Lucio's! I totally forgot! He's going to kill me!'

'Uh-oh,' Luke said. 'Tell him to try the black handkerchief pasta with cuttlefish and mussels. Love, love, love it.'

'Thanks for your culinary advice, Bill Granger, but I think you're missing the point here. This was supposed to be my I-know-I've-spent-more-time-getting-my-hair-extensions-changed-than-I've-spent-in-your-company-lately-but-let's-go-out-and-I-promise-I'll-make-it-up-to-you dinner. And I forgot!'

'Ah, take the chianti home in a doggy bag and give him a blow job,' Luke advised. 'Works for me all the time.'

I didn't have the time (or inclination) to ask whether he meant as the blower or blowee. I'd not even met Reuben yet, after all. Instead, I rolled my eyes, pocketed my insurance cheque and headed for the door, blowing air kisses back at Luke as I went. 'Sorry to love you and leave you, babe,' I shouted over my shoulder.

'Good luck, Jazzy Lou,' he called after me. I was gunna need it.

Flagging down a taxi on Victoria Street, I launched myself into the front seat and breathlessly directed the driver: 'To Windsor Street, Paddington, please. And step on it!' I'd always wanted to say that. Next I scrolled to Will's number, crossing myself as I hit dial. It was hardly Jewish but, hell, neither was Christmas and that had never stopped me. Holding my breath as the dial tone kicked in, I got . . . nothing. And not just by way of divine intervention. There was no response from Will either. Not a thing. He must have been ignoring me. You don't sit in a restaurant drinking chianti by yourself and not hear your phone ring. I shot him a text: *I am so, so sorry babe. B there in 5. Max. Save some vino for me xxx.*

As we sped up Victoria Street my mobile vibrated in reply. It was Will. *Don't bother,* was all he said.

Ouch.

I turned apologetically to the driver. 'Um, sorry. Change of plans. Can we head for Cascade Street instead, please?' It was time to go home. Ignoring Luke's sage advice about BJs, the only licking I planned to do tonight was of my own wounds. If by the expression 'licking wounds' you mean soaking in a bubble bath, drinking a cleanskin and watching reruns of *Gossip Girl*. Because that's where I was headed.

My phone buzzed again. Will: *Unless u want 2 skip dinner n just meet at my place?* I scrolled down to check there wasn't more. Something witty and loveable and vaguely boyfriend-like. Nothing. Unbelievable. What did he think I was, a St Kilda football club groupie? I hit delete and fumed quietly as we careered up Oxford Street. After spending my day in the office dodging the fire-breathing Diane, I did not have the energy for a showdown with Will tonight.

My phone went again. *Don't worry bout coming over. Ul only get here in time 2 have 2 turn round n leave in the middle of the nite on sum crazy mission for ur boss.* Well, that was just charming. Even if it was probably true. Taking a deep breath, I punched in my reply: *Look, I'm sorry I missed dinner. And I'd still like to see you tonight. But how bout we grab a drink at the London or somewhere near Lucios? Am in a taxi now and can b there super soon x*

'Sorry!' I turned back to the poor taxi driver. 'Scrap that! Better make it Windsor Street again.' By now we were careering down the back of Paddington, well past Lucio's and the London. Slamming on the brakes, the driver swung the car across the neat white lines down the middle of the road and headed back towards Windsor Street. He was wearing an expression I hoped was faint amusement, although I couldn't quite tell in the dark.

My mobile sprang to life again. It was Will: *Think I'll pass.*

Now, this was beyond. If I hadn't been secretly relieved to be off the hook, I'd be seriously pissed off by now. Fact is, I had a red-carpet event with sporting superstar Matthew Ashley tomorrow night and more than a sneaking suspicion Matt would test my mettle. He might have been a cricketer but this guy was better known for the speed with which he moved through bases. From first to fourth faster than an in-swinging googly, if you believed the tabloids. I'd need to be on the ball.

But back in the taxi my driver was going to kill me. 'Uh, you won't believe this,' I said, 'but I think we're heading for Cascade Street again. Sorry!' The tyres screeched once more as the cabbie swung the car around. This time no amount of darkness could shield me from his expression. 'Sorry,' I repeated sheepishly.

Then my phone buzzed again. It was Shelley: *Just opened that bottle of pinot gris if you're around. M-J is waiting for you . . . S x.* Oh, Marc Jacobs! Patron saint of disenfranchised women the world over! Who else could bring me back from the precipice of romantic doom but Marc Jacobs? I hit reply: *Hold that thought. And that corkscrew. Am on my way!*

Saint Marc, here I come.

'Actually, you'd better make that Woollahra,' I said to the driver. 'I can feel a conversion coming on.'

7

'Matt Ashley wants to be the male Paris Hilton of Sydney.'

This was according to Luke, who'd never met the guy. And while I couldn't claim to be a fan – of Matt Ashley or of cricket (hell, I couldn't pick a silly mid-off from a middle stump in a line-up) – I did think that was a bit unfair.

After all, just because you're blond and successful and in the public eye doesn't mean you're courting controversy. Or that you're vacuous. Or narcissistic. Or any of the other adjectives levelled at the Hilton heiress. So I was busy sticking up for Matt Ashley in a text war with Luke when I arrived at the Sydney Cricket Ground for tonight's event.

And then I met Matt.

'Hey, babe!' Matt Ashley lumbered over to introduce himself, all toothpaste-ad smile and boyish charm. This was the stuff to make any WAG melt.

'Hi, Matt, I'm Jasmine Lewis from Wilderstein PR. Great to meet you.' I stuck out my hand.

He swept me up in a bear hug, the sheer force of which briefly stopped the passage of air to my lungs. Asphyxiation by fast bowler. Awesome. You don't read that in a coroner's report every day.

'Great to meet you, babe,' Matt enthused. 'Geez, why is it all you PR chicks are hot? Is it in your job description or something?'

This was hardly a Shakespearean sonnet.

'Yeah, it's all part of our client care,' I said dryly, safe in the knowledge my sarcasm would miss its target. 'Now, I've got your publicity schedule here, Matt. The only timetabled interview tonight is with *Sports Daily* in half an hour. But *TVNN Sports* have a crew here so I'll try and get you some face time with them before the night's out. You've got your watch on, yeah?' Matt was the ambassador of Lacoste watches and Lacoste was the reason I was standing in the heritage-listed members' pavilion at the SCG. Lacoste was hardly our most lucrative client, but the fact they flew Diane to their team conference in Hong Kong twice a year, all expenses paid, seemed to cement their position eternally on our client list. Duty-free is Diane's favourite term, after bottom line.

'Oh, shit! My watch!' Matt swore, grabbing at his naked left wrist.

'No drama, I bought a spare,' I said chirpily, reaching into my handbag. I'd worked with sportsmen before.

Slapping the watch onto his arm, its warranty tag swinging on its band, Matt turned towards the Victorian red-cedar bar which was already heaving with bleached-blond pierced guys wearing the iconic green and gold.

'Getcha a drink, J?' Matt asked.

I shook my head. 'Not yet, thanks. I want to check in with *Sports Daily* in the media room. But I'll be back soon.' I added, 'Don't get into any trouble before then, okay?'

Matt winked and my stomach sank. 'Sure, babe,' he said, disappearing into the throng at the bar.

As I bumped my way towards the packed media room the eyes of cricketing greats stared down at me from every wall. This place screamed 'boys club' louder than a Cranbrook reunion. Turning the corner to step across the threshold and into the den of media, I was accosted by a guy wearing fashionable three-day growth and a pair of Tod's loafers. Hmm, this weren't no sports jock.

'PR flunkey?' he asked.

I spied a Canon camera in his hand, hidden casually behind the doorframe. 'Paparazzi,' I identified, smiling. 'What can I do for you, my photo-journalist friend?'

'You're Matt Ashley's minder, right?'

I hesitated. 'You mean his Public Relations and Media Strategist?' I corrected.

The pap grinned. 'Sure, whatevs. But you're here with Ashley, yeah?'

I hesitated again. 'How do you know that? I only met Matt five seconds ago.'

The pap laughed. 'You've never been worked over by a paparazzo before, have you, Flunkey? I've walked past you and the target five times already tonight and you still haven't got face recognition.'

The pap looked smug but the only word I heard in all that was 'target'. Matt was his target. 'You're after Matt Ashley tonight?' I asked excitedly. 'Fab!'

The pap looked mildly amused. 'Don't you even want to know why, Flunkey?'

I thought for a split second. 'No,' I said. 'Just make sure you get his left arm and his watch in all your shots.'

He shook his head. 'Shameless.'

I paused to ponder for a minute what it meant to be called shameless by a paparazzo. There is no tick-box for this on the 'What I want to be when I grow up' questionnaire they give you in careers guidance classes at high school. Nor can you enrol in 'Selling your soul 101' in your communications degree at Sydney Uni. An oversight, surely. Because it was at moments like these that I wanted to whip out a camera of my own, take a quick Polaroid, inscribe the back with *Career-defining moment #66* and add it to a montage on a cork board in my office at work. If only I had an office, that is.

Remembering I was meant to be tracking down *Sports Daily*, I swapped business cards with the pap and pushed inside. But not before I offered him some nice 'natural' shots with Matt during the evening. This, we both knew, was a promise to tip off this guy and his Canon just as soon as Matt was away from the crowds and in a position to be snapped unwittingly. After all, what self-respecting magazine runs a posed celebrity shot when there are paparazzi-style snaps on the table? As a PR, if you jump into bed with the paparazzi your product is guaranteed to be in print the next day.

'I'll be ready and waiting to get those shots. You just say the word, Flunkey,' he said as I left.

'Done, my paparazzi pal, done.' And I headed into the scrum of the media room.

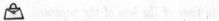

Later, back at the bar, two media interviews and three champagnes down, I was beginning to think the evening might actually be a success. Matt had provided the press with several column-inches' worth of sound bites. 'It was a team effort, we all gave a hundred and ten per cent and cricket was the winner on the day. By the way, have you got the time? Oh wait, let me check my new Lacoste watch.' Yada yada. But it was enough to keep me on the payroll for another day.

Plus, Matt and his teammates had waited till the end of the speeches before getting totally rollicking drunk. Some sort of record, I'm sure. In fact, the night was already winding to a close and their chants of 'Aussie, Aussie, Aussie, oi, oi, oi' had only been going relentlessly for, oh, about an hour or so now, much to the delight of the suits all around us.

Matt was just introducing me to yet another green-and-gold-clad bloke, this one roughly the height of a Harbour Bridge pylon, when I decided it was time to make a break for it.

'J, this is Brad, the other fast bowler,' Matt said.

'Nice to meet you, Brad, but I –'

'Hi there, Jay is it? Why are you PR chicks all so hot? Is it in your job description or something?' Brad asked.

Spare me. 'Actually, Brad, I'm afraid I was just leaving,' I said. I turned to Matt. 'Want a lift back to your hotel room, Matty?'

I hadn't meant for this to sound suggestive but Matt's face lit up like a tween at a Blue Light Disco. And I'm ashamed to say I didn't disabuse him of his delusion. *Whatever gets you out of here and in front of the lens of the paparazzi, bud.*

Grabbing Matt's hand for a speedy exit, I dragged him through the crowd of greying private-school boys and down the long flight of stairs towards the gates out the front. In my spare hand I clutched the paparazzo's business card and dexterously punched his number into my phone.

'Yeah?' he answered.

'It's your PR flunkey here,' I said quietly. 'Elvis is leaving the building.'

'Roger that,' he said, his tone immediately businesslike. 'Main entrance, Driver Avenue?'

'You got it,' I said, checking over my shoulder to ensure Matt couldn't hear me from where he trailed behind. 'Taxi,' I mouthed to Matt and indicated to my phone.

To my photographer friend I said, 'Oh, and left hand, remember? I need you to get that watch in the shot.'

'Got it,' he signed off.

As we approached the bottom of the staircase I dropped Matt's hand. Surely he could negotiate the final few stairs himself. He staggered towards the gates, looking more drunken sailor than professional cricketer, then paused and looked up at me with dopey, bloodshot eyes. 'Shit, J! I left my publishityschedule behind!' The words came out in a mush of slurred consonants, like a bad Sean Connery impersonation.

I tried to hurry Matt past the exit turnstiles. 'That's okay, Matty,' I said. 'You're almost done for the night. We've just got to get you out of here and into a taxi looking vaguely respectable and then I get to keep my job.'

As I said this, he slumped sideways into a wall. I was beginning to regret my call to the paparazzo.

'Whoa, up you get, bud,' I encouraged, reaching over to fix his baggy green cap, which was now dangling precariously off one ear, in a vain stab at making him look sober.

Big mistake.

As soon as I got close enough to him, Matt grabbed me by my arm and pushed me up against the wall, his beery mouth closing in over mine in a slobbery drunken kiss.

Oh. My. God.

'Are you mad?' I cried when he finally came up for air. I shoved at him but he only nuzzled up closer, his tongue sliding back into my mouth.

This was beyond revolting. I shoved again. Hard. 'What the fuck are you doing?' I cried when he paused for a second time. I ducked and left him pashing the brickwork, which gave me time to back away through the turnstile.

'J?' he asked, confused.

'Thanks, Flunkey!' came another voice.

Now I was confused. Gasping for air, I stumbled further away from Matt and caught sight of the person behind the second voice.

Fuck. My photographer friend. 'You didn't . . . that wasn't . . . did you?' I was struggling to find the words to form my sentence when I saw Matt coming back for round two. 'No, Matt!' I shouted, grateful for the turnstile between us. 'Stop!' I instructed desperately. Both to Matt and the pap.

Matt stopped in his tracks, looking hurt. 'J?'

I held up my hand in a stop signal as if training a dog. 'Stay there.'

Without waiting for a response, I ran over to where the pap and his camera had stood just seconds earlier. 'Where are you?' I called into the darkness. 'Hello?' And then, 'You better give me those pics right now!'

Nothing.

Turning again, I caught sight of him in the streetlights, bounding along the pavement, rapidly putting metres between him and the scene of the crime. He waved his camera in the air in thanks. Bastard. I was going to have to warn Diane. But first, I had Romeo to deal with. I stalked over to where Matt was slumped against the SCG ticket booth. *You're hardly gunna pull a crowd in that state, Matty,* I thought wryly to myself. I nudged him half-heartedly with my shoe as I considered the long line of eager taxis across the road. *Now, how do you suppose I get one drunk cricketer to cross the road?* I wondered. And why did my life so often sound like a bad joke? I reached for my phone while trying not to consider the punchline. It was time to call Diane.

But before I could phone in my own execution, my loving boyfriend did it for me. A text, sitting neglected in my inbox, greeted me as I slid open my phone. *Jazz*, it read, *I'm done. Will.*

Shit. Dumped by SMS. And before he even had the chance to see the happy snaps of me and Matt. I kicked the ticket booth and howled. 'I'm done too, Will. I'm done too.'

8

It's funny, I'd dedicated a lot of thought to leaving Wilderstein PR. I would spend hours at my desk dreaming up fantastic feats for terminating our relationship. Was a skywriter too much? I would ponder. A graffitied message on the Opera House a little unlawful? How about a banner on Anzac Bridge? As for the message, well, that was the easy part: OMG. It's you, not me. I quit, Diane. Pithy, professional but with a personal touch. Sadly, I never had the opportunity to put any of my master plans into action because Diane beat me to the punch.

The morning after my introduction to the gentleman's sport of cricket, I made my way to work. While I didn't expect a hero's welcome, nor did I expect the reception I got when I arrived. It seemed the tickertape parade hadn't yet kicked off as I stepped out of the lift at Wilderstein PR and slunk towards my desk. On my way I was careful to avoid all the glances around the office that were carefully avoiding me.

It was there, at my desk, that I was reacquainted with the events of last night. Reacquainted, that was, by way of my face smooshed up against Matt Ashley's mug and spread across a DPS in the Sun's gossip pages, under the banner BRASH ASH IN PASH AND DASH. Hilarious. The subbies at the Sun had been working overtime on that one. As had the smart-arse who had Blu-Tacked this fine piece of investigative journalism to the screen of my PC. At least the pap had managed to get Matt's watch in the shot.

I sat at my desk and idly waited for Diane's door to fly open and her ghoulish face to appear and order me into her office where she would shriek at me like a banshee. A custom that really was becoming tediously familiar. My groundhog day of being ground into submission. Still, the monotony of routine did nothing to calm the nerves in my stomach. Such a shame I was one of the few non-bulimics in fashion PR; butterflies like this would be a dream for regurgitation, surely. As I contemplated things that make you vomit, Diane appeared from nowhere, as if summoned by my very thoughts.

This was going to be ugly.

I stood, ready to follow Diane back to her lair for my disembowelment, but she was having none of that. She clicked her fingers at me and pointed to the floor to indicate I should stay where I was. This was going to be a public showdown. High noon and all that. I instinctively reached for where my gun holster should be.

'Oh. My. God,' she snarled, acronym abandoned in her fury. 'Never in my life have I been so humiliated.'

I didn't like to point out that it was my face plastered across this morning's tabloids like a Siamese twin to Gen Y's answer to Shane Warne.

'What do you have to say for yourself?' Heads swivelled as people gave up any pretence of not eavesdropping. A few stood for a better view.

'I didn't kiss Matt Ashley, Diane.' I knew I had limited time before the ole gunslinger pulled the trigger. I didn't intend to mince my words.

She arched an eyebrow so high it nearly flew off her Botoxed forehead.

'I didn't,' I persisted. 'He kissed me. Attacked me, actually. He was drunk. Very drunk. I managed to get him outside for a paparazzi shot for Lacoste and he pinned me to a wall.'

That eyebrow shot higher. It really was amazing how she got that much movement despite a truckload of botulinum.

'I see,' was all she said.

A ringing phone went unanswered somewhere as the whole office stayed glued to our contretemps. Tumbleweed rolled past.

'Pack up your desk, Jasmine,' she sighed, as though my being there and breathing the same air was draining for her. 'I can't have my publicists getting more headlines than my clients.'

I stared at her incredulously. Had she just fired me? Was I being sacked? My brain raced to catch up. I had never been fired in my life. I didn't know how to act fired. I was used to being promoted, or congratulated, or made McDonald's crew member of the month. Hell, I'd never even got a detention at school. I'd had far too earnest and middle-class a work ethic to wind up in detention. I had no prior experience of being fired and I wasn't sure I was up to it.

'I said I didn't kiss Matt Ashley!' I shouted like a petulant two-year-old. 'Don't you believe me?' I gesticulated wildly, throwing one unfortunate arm towards the Sun article like a game-show host pointing to the jackpot. Matt Ashley's tongue down my throat at 300 dpi resolution was perhaps not the best piece of evidence I could have picked to support my case. Good work, Calamity Jane.

Diane sighed her pained sigh again. 'Of course I believe you,' she snapped. 'It's not like Matt hasn't accosted one of my publicists before.'

My mouth fell open.

'But I'm afraid that's not the point, Jasmine.'

It wasn't?!

'The point is Lacoste are displeased with the coverage they've received, so heads must roll. Your head.'

My mouth stayed open. Someone was going to have to Hollywood tape my bottom jaw to its upper counterpart because it was going nowhere on its own.

Diane sighed one final time. 'Security will be here soon, Jasmine, to escort you from the premises.'

And with that, Diane Wilderstein turned on her Bally heel and stalked out of the saloon.

9

Following my sacking by Diane, my dumping by my boyfriend, my robbery, and my assault by an A-grade cricketer, I did what any self-respecting girl would do: I cried, I drank and I complained bitterly to anyone who would listen.

'It's not fair!' I wailed down the phone to Shelley. If she'd not heard this same line from me a thousand times already this week, she would have been forgiven for not being able to make out my words from where I sprawled prostrate in bed, a bag of full-fat, high-carb Black Star pastries by my side and a discarded empty wineglass on the floor, its telltale red-wine tide mark crusted like blood around the dirty rim. There'd been a lot of that going on lately. The bloody discarding of things, that is. (Although that could equally apply to the swigging of wine, I admit.) But it was the bloody discarding of things like me by that vampire Diane that was on my mind.

'All I did was get accosted by a client! People normally get compensation for such things. Not fired!' I whined.

'You should sue the bitch, dah-ling,' Shelley said soothingly.

I didn't disagree. In what was the closest I was going to get to a balanced diet since my sacking, I guzzled my friend's unflinching sympathy as hungrily as I guzzled cheap red wine. 'I would sue,' I replied, throwing my feet into the air to inspect my chipped toenail polish, 'but I can't afford to even google a lawyer, let alone hire one to act on my behalf.'

Shelley murmured in agreement. She was clearly preoccupied with something more interesting at her end. I couldn't blame her either. It was days now since I'd been made to pack up my desk at Diane's and take the long, lonely walk – flanked by security – to the building's glass-fronted entrance. Days since I'd proudly held my head high (and not just in order to see over the top of the cardboard box full of my worldly belongings that I was clutching). Days since I'd refused to cry, since I'd politely thanked the security guards for their company and since I'd walked stoically away from Wilderstein PR, confident in the utter injustice of it all. And stoic I'd remained. At least until I'd been a safe two blocks away and my arms had no longer been able to hold the weight of my box, when I'd promptly sat it down on the pavement, plonked myself on top and started – to my mortification – to cry.

'I would have cried too, love,' Luke consoled me when I recounted this to him afterwards, 'if I'd just tongued a sportsman.'

Anya's commiserations had been a little more sensitive. After all, she'd been there, done that and bought the T-shirt herself.

'Oh hon, you're better off out of Wilderstein PR. Truly,' she'd assured me.

This probably would have held more sway if Anya herself had, by now, secured a fabulous, high-paying publicist's job that involved her poaching all of Diane's clients and taking them out for dinner where they'd eat ludicrously expensive degustation meals courtesy of her new employer while bonding over the ridiculing of Diane's peccadilloes. As it was, Anya was still unemployed. The highlight of her fortnight was collecting her measly dole payment from Centrelink then going online to see what, if anything, she could still afford on MyCatwalk.com.

'Remind me again what it is you do as part of your work-for-the-dole services to qualify for unemployment benefits?' I asked Anya.

'I'm a mentor for underprivileged teens at my local high school,' she explained without irony. 'I teach them stuff like how to make their torn jeans work for this season. The distressed look never really went out, you know.'

I disguised my laugh with a cough. Only a fashion publicist could turn a government support requirement into a sartorial service.

Still, at least Anya was doing something proactive. I surveyed the mess of pastry crumbs and B-grade 1990s chick-flick DVDs in my orbit. Not to mention the empty cask of wine on my bedside table. That had been a mistake.

And apparently not the last one I was to make in my post-sacking slump. Nor the biggest.

Oh no. That honour went to my decision while still in my emotionally fragile, unemployed state to meet up with my now ex-boyfriend, Will, for the traditional post-breakup-exchanging-of-personal-belongings ritual. And what a mistake it was, on par with shoulder pads and mullets and Crocs and harem pants and 1980s perms – none of which should ever have had a moment in fashion history. And yet I went ahead in blissful ignorance and organised to meet Will at Raw Bar Japanese restaurant, just a stone's throw from Bondi Beach, so that we could be reacquainted with our own stuff and part ways with one another in a mature, adult fashion.

'Hi, babe.' I greeted Will with a kiss on each cheek, determined to be the bigger person as I slid into my seat in the corner of the restaurant.

'Hey, Jazzy Lou,' he responded. He looked pale and a little dishevelled, I noticed with satisfaction. Given I'd spent over two hours waxing my legs, painting my nails, applying makeup, blowdrying my hair and selecting then reselecting my outfit of a fabulous dégradé wool Stella McCartney jumpsuit, I felt I could take the moral high ground here. Career crisis or not, there was no excuse not to look hot.

'Sake?' Will asked.

I nodded.

We busied ourselves with the menu – a vast array of uncooked Asian delicacies. If my relationship was to be served up dead and cold on a slab, then so would be my food. I settled on salmon sashimi, with a side of seaweed salad.

'So, how have you been?' I asked, keen to deflect the conversation from my own situation.

'Good,' he replied in the customarily articulate style of the Australian male.

'I brought your stuff.' I indicated a bag by my feet crammed with T-shirts and CDs and a camera and other odd remnants of our relationship.

'Same,' he said and pointed to a green recycling bag on the seat next to him.

I nodded awkwardly.

'So, Matt Ashley, huh?' Will asked, trying to feign indifference.

Will must have seen the tabloid pic of Matt Ashley with his tongue down my throat. (I didn't dwell, here, on exactly how many other people across greater Sydney were likely to have spied it too.)

'OMG! No!' I cried in horror. 'Oh no! No way!'

Polite Japanese waitresses looked over at me nervously. *Who is this crazy blonde girl and will she make a mess in our restaurant?* their immaculate expressions said.

'No way,' I repeated for emphasis. 'Matt Ashley and I . . . that was not . . . that was a mistake.'

Will raised a sceptical eyebrow and sipped his sake.

'Really,' I persisted. 'It wasn't what it looked like. I mean, yes, Matt did kiss me but it wasn't wanted. Or reciprocated.' How many times was I destined to have this conversation? 'It was just work,' I added lamely.

At the mention of work Will's dark eyes flashed and I knew I'd stepped on a landmine. I popped edamame beans and waited for Will's explosion.

'Yeah, I know all about your work, Jazzy Lou,' he started. 'I heard a lot more about your career than I did about anything else during the whole time we dated.'

I bit down on my soy bean, hard.

'Only, mostly I heard about it when you were telling me you couldn't make it to dinner because you were working back. Or you were missing another party because some C-grade celeb needed babysitting. Or you had to skip my birthday because your boss broke a nail.'

This last comment made me cringe. It was true that I'd missed Will's birthday dinner, but the reason why eluded me now. Sure, his broken-nail comment was spiteful, but I couldn't be sure that my no-show wasn't Diane-related. It certainly sounded plausible.

'In fact,' Will went on, getting warmed up as our clinically cold meal arrived, 'I can't quite believe you found time in your schedule to meet me tonight. Don't tell me the wheels of Wilderstein PR are turning without you for a whole evening? Surely there's a product launch or a premiere of something you should be attending?'

I grimaced into my gohan.

'No? Not got a runway you should be side of stage for?'

'Actually, no,' I replied, steeling myself. 'I no longer work for Wilderstein PR.'

Will threw his head back and laughed heartily. 'You're not working for Diane?' he asked incredulously. 'But that place is your life, Jazz!'

I blinked hard as I pretended this didn't hit home. 'Not any more,' I said haughtily. I could feel my impersonation of a functioning, coping member of society growing wobbly. I shouldn't have come here tonight. Seeking closure on my relationship with Will so soon after my career sought closure from me was just too much to handle. 'Wilderstein PR was not my life!' I lied. 'I don't need that job and I don't need you!'

I grabbed the bag by my feet and thrust it at Will, knocking the bowl of edamame beans everywhere in my haste. The bright, bouncing beans escaped across the table in a flurry of salt and spilled sake. Will looked shocked. The waitresses looked horrified.

I swiped my own bag of possessions from where it sat glumly beside Will.

'I've moved on from Wilderstein PR and I've moved on from you,' I announced. Then I turned on my heel and stalked out into the warm beachside air.

Days after my disastrous dinner with Will, I decided it was time to bite the bullet.

'I'm going to start that PR business I told you about,' I said to Luke one afternoon over a particularly rancid glass of goon, the only alcohol my redundant self could now afford.

Luke eyed me dubiously. I could see his brain oscillating between wanting to shoot me down in flames and being too scared to disagree with the crazy girl who had finally stopped crying for the first time in a fortnight. He opted for the latter.

'Really? That's *amaze*, babe.' He slugged some wine to wash down his insincerity.

'I'm serious,' I said.

Luke put down his glass. 'Jazzy Lou, has this got anything to do with the fact your only claim to fame at dinner with Will last weekend was the fact you inadvertently pashed an A-grade cricketer? An accidental kiss that doesn't gloss over the fact you're single and unemployed and have fallen off the coping wagon?'

Ouch. With friends like these, who needs enemies? I'd seen daytime television interventions that were less harsh.

'No,' I lied. 'And, anyway, I didn't bring up Matt Ashley, Will did. He backed me into a corner.'

'That so?' asked Luke. 'Would that be the corner you were cowering in when you turned kamikaze and threw food and wine all over the joint before storming out? Can we ever eat at Raw again?'

I sighed in response.

'Jazzy Lou, you know I want you to succeed more than anyone else in the world, right?' Luke said, more gently now. 'And I'd love you to start your own PR business. If only so you can give me an exclusive with all your famous clients.'

This was more like it.

'But,' he went on, 'you can't just go off and start your own company because you had a fight with your ex. Or because Diane sacked you. God, if everyone did that the ASX would go under from the demand for newly registered companies. Diane's track record for firing employees puts Donald Trump in the shade. You can't let her get to you.'

'It's not just because of Diane,' I lied again, visualising running a Public Relations Golden Target Award trophy inscribed with my name through Diane's heart.

Luke topped up my glass. 'But what about the master plan, Jazzy? You know, earn your stripes, learn the ropes, and do all those other corporate clichés before you branch out on your own?'

I scowled.

'Jazz,' Luke reasoned, 'you've only got a thirteen-thousand-dollar insurance cheque and an unhealthy collection of OPI nail polishes to your name. If the dwindling remainder of your savings wasn't paying your rent, you'd be on the street right now. Exactly how do you plan to fund this business venture?'

If Luke was trying to change my mind he was going about it the wrong way. Nothing says 'do' to a Jewish woman louder than saying 'don't'. Hell, we made the Bar Mitzvah Disco apparel line fashionable. If anyone could create a company out of nothing it was me. Either that or go crazy trying.

Recognising this, Luke resigned himself to my fate. 'So what will you call this conglomerate of yours?' he asked.

I stared at him incredulously. How did he know I'd already thought of a name? 'Queen Bee PR.'

If I was going to put up with all the aggro involved in being head honcho of my own company, then I wanted everyone to know who was boss. Regal, powerful and with a sting in the tail if you didn't fall into line, that would be my management approach. And naturally it made sense to call the company after me, the Queen Bee.

I did, however, mentally file my folder full of company logo designs in the bottom drawer of my mind. Just for the minute anyway.

Luke laughed. 'No funding, no business plan, no premises, but a name. I admire your style, Lewis.'

I raised my wine-stained glass in the air. Mazel tov to that, my friend. Mazel tov to that.

10

Over the coming months I worked like a madwoman to get Queen
Bee PR up and buzzing. I cashed in my insurance cheque. I wrote
a business plan and comprehensive SWOT analysis. I begged the
bank for finance. I rewrote my business plan and comprehensive
SWOT analysis. I secured my requested finance. I then drank a
bottle of Bollinger (purchased with said finance). I got an ABN.
I got an accountant. And I stopped buying Bollinger. I contacted
all my local real estate agents about renting office space. None of
them called me back. I invested in subscriptions to Media Monitors
and Margaret Gee's online. I created a publicity database, a press
release template, a PR protocol and a publicity schedule pro forma.
I set up a Queen Bee website and blog and Facebook page and
Twitter account so I never once had to stop working. And I never
once stopped working. I bought my PCs in bulk and second-hand.

I returned my PCs when Shelley insisted on buying me brand-new Macs. I owed Shelley a world of debt. (This in addition to the world of debt I owed my bank.) I stopped lunching with Luke at expensive restaurants. But I continued drinking cheap vino with Luke in quantities that were no good for my liver. Frustratingly, I still hadn't heard from any real estate agents. I lost hours on the kikki.K website looking at colour-coordinated stationery. I met with my accountant again. I ordered no-name stationery in mismatched colours. I looked into insurance (fire, storm, malicious damage, legal liability, business interruption, personal injury and property damage). I nearly died of boredom. I rang the still-unemployed but ever-reliable Anya (who was trawling eBay for Raven's stolen knickers at the time) and offered her a job. I drank Bollinger with Anya when she said yes. I promised to start paying her just as soon as I started making money. I finally heard from the real estate agent and was pleasantly surprised when he a) turned out to be hot, and b) started showing me potential office spaces. I developed a marketing plan. I redeveloped a Nurofen habit. I fell in love with the Vivienne Westwood tartan leather laptop case Shelley gifted me. I researched my industry competitors. I assessed my market appeal. I continued to view depressingly expensive warehouse spaces. I began looking for, pitching for and begging for clients. I started advertising for publicists to join the company. I slept with my too-temptingly-cute real estate agent. Suddenly I started being shown amazing office spaces. I had a business logo designed. I rented out an au courant warehouse in Alexandria (if warehouses can be au courant). I registered my business name as a trademark. I made a voodoo doll of Diane. I began to receive calls from potential clients. I received a 'congratulations' present from Luke in the form of a red Vixenary g-string. (Hilarious.) I worked too many hours. I slept too few. I went on the occasional doomed date. I received the odd phone call from my concerned parents asking why I'd dropped off the face of the earth. I let them go to message bank. I had the warehouse fitted out. I started interviewing potential employees. I began drinking in earnest. I spent weeks looking at paint swatches with Luke for the office fitout. I ignored Luke's interior decorating advice then immediately regretted it. I repainted the office myself at the weekend. I burned through the contacts list in my BlackBerry trying to drum up business. I schlepped to a thousand meetings all over Sydney to pitch to potential clients. I had business cards printed. I signed on my very first client. I celebrated with Bollinger in the office with my close friends. I didn't invite my accountant. I began attending launches and any other red-carpet event Luke could sneak me into in the hope of picking up new clients (I was dressed exclusively by Shelley for all red-carpet events). I began attracting more clients. I hired two additional publicists to keep Anya company. I continued to work too many hours. I continued to sleep too few. I nearly had a nervous breakdown. But I secured even more work. I splurged on Matt Blatt suspension lights. I avoided calls from my accountant. I stopped taking Luke's decorating advice in the form of Matt Blatt lights. I lost weight. I looked haggard. My dates kept ending disastrously. I worked even harder. I heard a rumour Diane was appalled that I'd started my own PR company. I celebrated with champagne for my staff of three (and this time I invited the accountant). I still didn't throw out my Diane voodoo doll. I didn't take a holiday. I never turned off my phone. I checked my emails relentlessly. I woke up at three on the dot each morning and rechecked them. I started making money. I had more desks brought into the office. I hired a receptionist called Lulu. I continued traipsing all over the greater metropolitan area seeking business. I started making some real money. I started returning my accountant's calls. I was lunching with Luke again. I was still working all hours of the day and night but it was beginning to pay off. I began to think I might actually make this thing work – if only we could continue to keep our head above water. I moved out of my old rented apartment and got myself a mortgage of my own. I bought myself an Aston Martin. I received bad press over my Aston Martin. But I continued to get the very best press for my clients. Then finally, finally, I celebrated my first anniversary at Queen Bee PR. And celebrated it in style.

'Jasmine will be here in eight minutes!' a panicked voice called.

I paused on the concrete front steps of the Queen Bee warehouse in Alexandria, in the industrial but up-and-coming outskirts of inner Sydney. I checked my watch. No one had told it we still had eight minutes to go.

Beyond the heavy glass door in front of me – inside QB HQ – I could see a flurry of flustered activity as the Bees raced to get ready for tonight's first-anniversary party.

'She texted to say she was in a taxi and on her way back from the salon,' the voice continued, 'so we need to make sure all those gift bags are ready or she's going to freak!'

I hesitated at the door. It was true I'd just left the salon where I'd had an emergency blowdry after a long day of organising, booking, confirming, rearranging, rebooking, reconfirming and general bossing of everyone in my vicinity ahead of tonight's event. It was also true that I'd texted the Bees to say the boss would be there on the hour and now I'd turned up eight minutes early. But most of all it was true that if I walked through the glassy entrance to Queen Bee and found the gift bags for tonight's special guests (including media) not quite ready, I. Would. Definitely. Freak.

I took a deep breath before buzzing myself in and ploughed on into the grand curved reception area where *Queen Bee* was emblazoned in hot-pink scrawl on the otherwise minimalist warehouse wall. A chandelier the size of a small Pacific island hung grandly above the reception desk. You could never accuse me of subtlety. Inside, the showroom was like an Aladdin's cave of fashion, with nearly fifty clothing rails lined up in rows, each bearing the latest in designer threads. We received two clothing drops in summer (summer and then cruise), followed by a third drop in winter, so there was never a shortage of couture collecting about the place. The shelves around the showroom were jam-packed with accessories, each shelf dedicated to a single salient item. There was a shelf for gloves and a shelf for hats, a shelf for scarves and a shelf for watches. Hell, we even had space dedicated to thongs in summer and ugg boots in winter. Shoes of every colour and description sat on display around the room. In the far corner of the open-plan sprawl lay a treasure trove of cosmetics and beauty products. The A to Z of beauty bliss, everything from Aveda to Za. A beauty editor could die and go to heaven in there. In fact, all we needed was a cash register and somewhere to swipe our fashionistas' hard-working Amex cards and the place really could have passed for a very stylish department store.

'Gah!' I exclaimed, barging into the warehouse-slash-office-space and causing unprepared Bees around the room to jump. 'Since when are salads on the menu for tonight?' I bent over the reception desk where a selection of platters for this evening's party had recently been delivered. Platters containing row upon neat row of Asian salads, each laid out in a glossy little white takeaway box. I picked up a chopstick that lay on the platter and poked one of the offending salads, turning it over in its box to check it was similar all the way through. Disastrous.

Surrounding the greens was the remainder of the food we had ordered for this evening. Food far more fitting for the theme of 'sweet success'. There were luridly coloured lollies and lollipops and candy canes and popcorn served in vintage cardboard boxes, as if begging to be taken to the Saturday matinee flicks. There were sherbets and musk sticks and Jaffas and Freckles and Jelly Snakes in every colour of the rainbow.

Then there were the salad leaves.

'Why are there healthy alternatives contaminating my preservatives?' I shouted. Honestly, this was the problem with being the boss of your own company. No one else paid anywhere near the same attention to details as you. No one else could be trusted to get things absolutely perfect.

Emma abandoned her post where she was tying ribbons onto gift bags and headed over to placate me. 'That's my fault, Jazz,' she began.

I braced myself. Emma was one of the very first Bees I'd recruited when I kicked off the business twelve months ago, and her job title could be loosely classified as publicity Girl Friday. Only, because this business never stops, never sleeps, never pauses to even draw breath, Em's role was more like 'Girl Every Second of Every Day'.

'When the caterer called to confirm the order,' Emma continued, 'I thought it sounded like a lot of sugar for a bunch of fashionistas, so I added some salads.'

I groaned. 'Em! The only green at this event should be on the rainbow-coloured gobstoppers. Tonight Snap and Crackle can get stuffed because we're all about *Pop!* Think kitsch, think colour, think Katy Perry on crack.'

Emma nodded in understanding.

'And anyway, we don't need to worry about providing low-fat options,' I added. 'This is a fashion-industry event. No one's actually going to *eat* the food. Most of the people here tonight won't have consumed calories since the mid-eighties when the Amazonian look was last in. Send the salads back,' I admonished.

Em nodded again and I left her to wrangle with the witlof while I inspected the rest of the preparations.

Over in the far corner my remaining three Bees were putting the final touches on tonight's gift bags, snakes of satin ribbon slithering on the floor around them. 'Anya! Alice! Lulu!' I shouted, addressing each employee in turn. 'Those goodie bags are looking great!'

The Bees glowed at the praise.

Since joining Queen Bee, Anya had proven herself a much more capable publicist than she'd ever been given credit for at

Wilderstein PR and, as such, was now responsible for handling several of our key accounts, with some great media coverage to show for it. Alice was the junior publicist in the office but what she lacked in experience she more than made up for with her edgy style. And QB receptionist Lulu brought enthusiasm to each crazy mission her boss set her. Like this one, for instance.

'Queen Bee is renowned for the best damn gift bags in the industry, so let's make sure our first-anniversary bags are bigger and better than ever,' I said. 'I want these bags to have *style*. I want these bags to have *panache*. When our guests receive their gift bag tonight they should feel like they're being bestowed a store bag from Chanel on Castlereagh: classy yet classic.'

'But cardboard?' complained Lulu as the goods in one over-stuffed bag sagged through the bottom and onto the floor.

I ignored her. 'Just make sure the satin bow is on the non-creased side of the bag and the custom-made tissue paper inside is folded not scrunched.' I dusted the mess from Lulu's collapsed bag off my Louis Vuitton two-piece number.

Anya, Alice and Lulu got back to work while I headed upstairs onto our rooftop terrace, the scene for tonight's celebrations.

Here, under a perfect Sydney sunset, among the fairy lights and the candy-store trimmings, was a wonderland of pop-coloured excess. Bunting flags zigzagged across the rooftop garden, which was decorated lavishly with oversized glass jars brimming with sugar-coated sweets. Giant gingerbread men stood sentry by the doorway, where they would usher guests into the hyperglycaemic haven that lay beyond. Trays of fruity cocktails dotted every available surface. And there, in the centre of the terrace, stood the icing on our anniversary cake: a giant ice sculpture in the shape of the Queen Bee logo over which sweetened vodka flowed like water. It was better than any land of milk and honey up here.

I sighed with contentment and adjusted the banner reading: Queen Bee 1st Anniversary, *The taste of sweet success.*

Everything was just as it should be. Tonight I, Jazzy Lou, former minion to Diane Wilderstein, would celebrate my first year in business as the boss of my very own PR company. I liked the taste of that.

And to help me celebrate in style we'd invited the who's who of A-listers, fashionistas and media influencers. Names like Pamela Stone, the undisputed gossip queen of Sydney, who was always first with the inside. So fast was Pamela with finding out the latest, she made Gossip Girl look like a piece of string between two tin cans. Also making the cut tonight was Lillian Richard, editor of *Eve Pascal* women's magazine. Lillian might have been last in line when it came to hair care but she was third in line in the Richard media dynasty and a very powerful ally to have in glossy magazines. Of course we had to invite up-and-coming design sensation – and Queen Bee's star client – Allison Palmer. Plus there was Samantha Priest too. An occasional model, frequent socialite and constant bogan, Priest would do all that was unholy to resurrect her flagging career, but the Sydney social pages – and a Queen Bee celebration – wouldn't be complete without her.

But tonight's event was not solely about Queen Bee savouring its one-year anniversary. Oh no, this was only the beginning, my friends. You see, we might have just survived our first twelve months in business, but PR was a fickle world and Sydney fashion

PR provided an especially slippery slope. One false move, one lost client, and our still-fledgling fashion firm could find itself suddenly so last season. And I, more than anyone, was acutely aware of the precariousness of our situation.

With this in mind I had come up with a plan that would have Sydney eating out of our hand: Kitchen Divas.

Let me explain. Kitchen Divas was reality TV meets foodie heaven. This all-girl cook-off was a weekly television ratings winner. In the city where your barista is more intimate with your preferences than your significant other could ever hope to be, Kitchen Divas guaranteed success. And not just success for the show itself but also for those lucky enough to be close enough to bask in the warmth of its kitchen blowtorch glow.

Which was why I'd invited Belle Single along to our birthday bash tonight.

Single, Shire high priestess and aspiring actress, also happened to be an upcoming contestant on the new season of Kitchen Divas. I didn't have high hopes for Belle in the kitchen. Hell, she'd probably never cooked a meal in her life. What I was counting on was this blonde being a firm favourite with Kitchen Divas fans. And when she was? Well, Belle would need representation. Who else would make sure her acting career bubbled along nicely while she took time out to promote her new cookbook and flog her stainless-steel saucepan range?

Naturally, when I'd heard that Belle Single had recently sacked her publicist, I'd taken the liberty of approaching her and talking her through exactly what it was that Queen Bee could do to publicise her upwardly mobile career. And she'd certainly sounded interested in that. Interested enough to come along to our first birthday soirée. Now all that was left for me to do was to convince Belle to sign on the dotted line of a binding contract making Queen Bee PR her exclusive public relations agency of choice. And when better to do that than at a party celebrating our success in the Sydney scene? In one swift move I would provide Belle with a publicity team just in time for the new season of *Kitchen Divas* and at the same time guarantee Queen Bee's survival for at least another year to come.

If only Diane Wilderstein were here to chew on this, I thought smugly.

My phone buzzed in my hand.

'Lulu?' I answered.

'Jazzy Lou, the first of our guests have arrived so I've sent them straight up to the terrace,' she replied.

I checked my watch. 'Who the hell has arrived so unfashionably on time?' I asked as the terrace door sprung open behind me.

'Jasmine,' came an all-too-familiar voice. A voice dripping with money and malice.

'Diane!' I gasped.

Her skinny silhouette joined her voice on the rooftop. 'How delightful to be the first to your little party,' she sneered.

My mind was spinning as I raced to catch up. Diane was here? At Queen Bee PR? To celebrate the success of my first year in business? This didn't make any sense. I steadied myself on an oversized candy cane.

'I do hope more people show up, don't you?' she asked, faux concern dripping from her faux lips.

I stammered a reply. 'Of course more people will show up,' I hissed. 'People such as *invited guests.*'

As if to prove my point, Belle Single chose this moment to step out onto the terrace.

'Belle Single!' I gushed, racing over to the stylish blonde. 'So glad you could make it!' I shot Diane a pointed look.

Belle air-kissed both my cheeks. 'Jasmine!' she said. 'This place is *amaze!*' She looked around the rooftop with admiration. 'It looks like Willy Wonka's visited up here!'

'It looks like Willy Wonka's *vomited* up here,' Diane corrected.

I considered stabbing her with the nearest candy cane.

'It really is very Ken Done of your decorator,' Diane added evilly as I steered Belle away from the Ice Queen and over to the ice luge, where newly arrived guests were beginning to gather to get a drink.

'Vodka?' I asked Belle, pressing a glass of the sickly-sweet alcohol into her hand.

She nodded by way of reply.

'Now, don't worry about Diane,' I assured her. 'She just doesn't appreciate a food theme like we do here at Queen Bee.'

The Kitchen Diva smiled cryptically as more people spilled out onto the terrace around us.

'In fact, we often create amazing events for our clients based solely around the catering.'

'We can theme product launches around food from particular regions or eras or to match fashion trends or moods,' I went on, attempting to appeal to her (very) inner foodie and show her Queen Bee was just the right fit for her new foray into the kitchen.

'And recently,' I added, 'we organised a fab vampire-themed launch where all the food was black. Not burned,' I hurried on as she appeared to stifle a laugh. 'Just black. Gothic. It's amazing what you can do with food colouring and a little . . .' My voice trailed off.

Belle sipped lazily from her glass and was now gazing round the growing party in search of a distraction.

I made one last stab. 'Belle, have the producers of *Kitchen Divas* started talking product placement with you yet? I could sit in on some of the meetings and give my thoughts if you're looking for support.'

Belle simply offered a smile.

'Thanks, Jasmine,' she said at last. 'We'll see,' she added half-heartedly before turning and heading into the crowd, leaving me alone next to the vodka flow with only a sinking feeling for company.

Thank fuck Luke and Shelley chose this moment to make their appearance and join the rapidly growing throng of revellers.

'Mazel tov, dah-ling!' Shelley called, waving wildly as she and Luke made their way through the madding crowd and met me at the ice sculpture in the middle of the terrace. 'Fabulous do,' she added as she bypassed the dainty cocktail glasses on offer and instead picked up a large water glass and thrust it in the stream of vodka.

'Totes!' agreed Luke, chewing as he spoke, his mouth already stuffed full of sugar. 'This is incred, Jazzy Lou!'

I smiled in gratitude and tried to push my worries about Belle Single to the back of my mind. 'Thanks, loves,' I said. 'Did you see the edible gingerbread house in the corner? Only don't taste it – it cost me a bloody fortune.'

Luke pointed to his mouth as if to indicate there wasn't a whole lot of room in there right now, anyway.

'Nice styling,' Shelley commented, referring to my LV ensemble that was on loan from her. Naturally the two-piece was totally new season but it wouldn't matter if Shell had owned it for ten years, she never would have fitted into it. (Although I'd never point that out to her.)

'Ta babe,' I said instead. 'And likewise.' I was referring to the glam Roberto Cavalli silk-chiffon maxi she was wearing.

'And *moi*?' said Luke, holding the side panels of his Dolce & Gabbana coat open to reveal the bright red plaid inside.

'You look beyond,' I assured him. 'Good enough to eat. Speaking of – where's Reuben?' Luke's squeeze was a pastry chef and would have loved tonight's foodie theme.

Luke looked glum. 'Working,' he said.

'Shame,' I replied, keeping one eye firmly on what was happening around us as I spoke.

'That's okay. I can be your beau for this evening. That is, of course, unless you've got someone special here tonight already? No Mr Jazzy Lou you'd like to introduce us to?' he asked, giving Shelley a nudge.

I rolled my eyes. 'Not that I've received the memo about,' I said. 'And that's about the only way I'll ever have time to meet a boy – if he comes to me on an office memo.'

Shelley groaned and refilled her already empty glass. 'Babe, you need to work less and bonk more already. Have you even seen anyone since you humiliated yourself in front of Will at Raw Bar last year?'

I grimaced at the memory. 'Uh, kinda,' I stalled, thinking of my brief liaison with the real estate agent who had found me the Queen Bee office space. Nothing like mixing a little business with pleasure, I say. Not that I have much choice. When your entire life is dedicated to business you squeeze in the pleasure where you can.

'Kinda?' Shelley echoed, obviously not satisfied.

'Yeah, kinda. I – OMFG! Is that Lillian Richard talking to Diane?!' I interrupted myself, ending all further investigation into my life between the sheets.

'Diane?!' Luke shrieked, hearing only the key word in that sentence. 'What the hell is she doing here?'

'I have no idea!' I matched his shriek and several people looked in our direction. 'But I intend to find out! Right before I throw her out.'

Shelley and Luke exchanged worried glances. 'Er, I'm not sure that's a good idea, Jazzy Lou,' Shelley started.

Luke jumped in. 'It's not, Jazz. Sure, Diane's not here to help you blow out the candles on your anniversary cake, but chucking her out will only cause a scene. A scene you'll read about in tomorrow's paper.'

I glanced at him quickly for signs of his notepad. Not that it mattered. Even if Luke managed to convince his editor it wasn't worth running, any public altercation I had with Diane at my anniversary event was sure to earn ink elsewhere. It was a fast fall from sweet success to bad taste, after all.

I took a deep breath before conceding to myself that they were right. 'Fine,' I huffed. 'But I can still find out why she's here. That and prevent her from poaching my press contacts.' And with that I stomped off in Diane and Lillian's direction.

When I approached Diane that evening she was deep in conversation with magazine deity Lillian Richard.

'Lillian!' I interrupted, barging in on their cosy chat and bumping Diane into an oversized lollipop nearby. 'Good to see you could squeeze us into your schedule for tonight.'

Diane scowled at me. I flashed a saccharine smile in response.

Lillian stuck out her hand in her usual businesslike manner, her wild-woman hair bobbing around her face like a mane. 'Good to be here, Jasmine,' she said. 'Queen Bee certainly knows how to throw a party.'

I threw Diane a triumphant look. She looked like she wanted to throw me off the edge of the terrace.

'Thank you, Lillian,' I replied graciously, raising my champagne flute in reply. 'After twelve months of hard slog getting the business up and running, we thought a party was well deserved. Especially for our friends in the industry who have helped us along the way.'

'Quite,' Lillian agreed and took a sip of pink champagne. 'There's nothing like the feeling of letting your hair down after all that hard work.'

I hoped Lillian didn't plan to let that hair down. There simply wasn't space on the terrace.

'Exactly!' I said pointedly. 'Tonight is all about celebrating hard work that's done and dusted. Only, you're not here on new business tonight, are you, Diane?' I wheeled around to clock her reaction but the she-devil didn't flinch.

'Quite the opposite,' she beamed falsely. 'Lillian and I were just arranging a dinner party at her home for next weekend.'

I choked on my pink champagne. 'Dinner party? How lovely,' I managed through gritted teeth. 'I had no idea you two were close friends?'

'Very,' said Diane emphatically. 'You'd just never guess who's connected to who in this industry.'

Now it was my turn to scowl. What the hell was that supposed to mean? I took a gulp of my drink before replying, 'You just never would, would you?'

At the mere mention of industry connections, gossip queen Pamela Stone appeared by my side, as if somehow summoned by Diane's cryptic comment and the promise of a juicy story behind it. I swear that woman could smell gossip. I only hoped her sixth sense would be put off tonight by the sickly smell of artificial additives filling the air. That way, she wouldn't detect my deepening suspicions about why Diane was here. A scandal of that type at my anniversary party was one gossip column I didn't care to see in print.

'Gals!' Pamela addressed us collectively, despite the good twenty years separating me from Diane and Lillian. 'Have you tasted this divine fairy floss? It looks like the naughtiest thing, dolls, but the inside? Just air!'

I smiled at Pamela, grateful for the distraction. Much as I tried to remind myself tonight was a celebration, I couldn't help stewing on Diane's undoubtedly evil plans. I only had to *consider* for a fleeting moment the possibility that Belle Single's lucrative account might be slipping through my fingers and I felt sick to my stomach.

'Now, dolls,' Pamela said to Diane and me between multicoloured mouthfuls, 'what do you make of Belle Single being sans spin doctor? Such an opportunity, isn't it? Will either of you be stepping up to the publicity plate to represent her?'

I groaned inwardly as Pamela outed the elephant in the room. In one fell swoop this boss of goss had ruined any plans I had for a quiet takeover of Belle's account by discussing it in front of the very last person in the world I wanted her to: Diane.

For the millionth time tonight I wished the ground would open up and swallow Diane Wilderstein, taking her far, far away from my party and my plans for *Kitchen Divas* world domination.

Turned out I was not the only one. As Pamela's question hung unanswered in the air and I turned expectantly to face Diane, I caught sight of the very last thing in the world I had ever expected to see: Diane blushing. She was actually blushing. And while it was hardly a shade to rival the popping-pink of Pamela's fairy floss, the colour of embarrassment was undeniably spreading across Diane's face.

Sprung.

Pamela, not one to miss a story, saw it too. 'OMG, Diane,' she exclaimed triumphantly, 'don't tell me you've already snapped up the beautiful Belle Single? Can I confirm that? What about a quote from you? And let's line up a pic of you with Belle, shall we?'

As Pamela raved and I reeled, Diane looked on, any signs of embarrassment replaced by smug delight. In fact, if Pamela and Lillian hadn't been there to witness the fleeting blush, I'm not sure I would really have believed Diane had expressed such a human emotion.

'Well, Diane, you've really blown me away with this scoop,' continued Pamela as she scrounged through her handbag for a notepad and pen.

Yeah, you and the competition, I thought desperately.

Fuck.

No wonder Belle Single had struggled to keep a straight face when I'd pitched my heart out to her earlier. She was already in bed with Diane and the two of them were having a good old laugh at my attempts at a *ménage à trois.*

Fuck.

Belle and Diane must have been planning this for weeks. All that time I'd been killing myself coming up Queen Bee's publicity campaign for her career, she'd probably been feeding my proposals straight to Diane.

Fuck.

And tonight – my first-year anniversary of all nights – was when they planned to reveal their alliance. Why else would Belle agree to come if she had no intention of signing with Queen Bee? And what other excuse could Diane have for crashing our birthday bash? None. She just wanted to maximise my suffering.

Fuck.

Belle Single was to be the biggest signing of Queen Bee's short existence. Without her, our future looked far less rosy. Sure, we still had plenty of other clients, enough to keep the debtors from the door for the next few months at least. But signing Belle Single at her *Kitchen Divas* zenith was a recipe for a whole new level of PR success. Success we might never taste now.

The rest of the evening passed in a sickly-sweet blur. Celebs floated by, drunk on vodka and E-numbers, as I struggled to keep one eye fixed firmly on Diane and her accomplice. I was standing beside a flock of fashionistas who were posing by giant-sized lollipops that probably weighed more than they did, when Emma approached, schedule in hand.

'Jazzy Lou, it's nearly time to cut the cake,' she read from the running order I'd put together for this evening, which divided the event into seven-minute increments.

'Already?' I replied distractedly, even though I'd checked the schedule myself only moments earlier. I scanned the rooftop again for signs of sabotage from Diane.

'Totes,' Em confirmed. 'Speech then cake then directions for gift-bag pick-up for guests. All in the next twenty-three and a half minutes, according to your timeline.'

I sighed and gave up on Diane for a moment. 'Twenty-three and a half minutes?' I echoed. 'We'd better get cracking then.' I snapped into the work mode. 'Is the cake on a platter and ready to go? I'll assemble the photogs now if you get the cake to the terrace. And tell Lulu and Alice to do a final check of the gift bags, while Anya should start rounding up the crowd for the cake. Got it?'

Em nodded, then buzzed off to find the other Bees, her clipboard still firmly in hand.

Twelve and a half minutes later, in accordance with the schedule, I signalled for the DJ to kill the music and took my place centre stage in front of the brightest and most beautiful Sydney's fashion and PR industries had to offer. A giant first-anniversary cake by my side. Standing all around me were the faces of those I loved (or, at least, loved to work with). Luke and Shelley, Pamela and Lillian, the Bees, clients, media and industry types. Then there was Diane, standing in front of Hansel and Gretel's gingerbread house like the wicked witch. I instinctively reached for the cake knife.

The DJ hit mute and the candles on the cake were lit. Emma, who was standing directly in my line of sight as a prompt in case I needed it, subtly raised her clipboard and tapped one manicured fingernail against the running order tacked on there; 9.17 pm: *Speech from Queen Bee*, her fingernail indicated. I nodded and willed myself to look at the assembled crowd and not to be distracted by Diane.

'Family and friends of Queen Bee PR,' I began, 'we're buzzed you could join us for an evening of decadence, debauchery and, quite possibly, diabetes as we celebrate our first anniversary.' The assembled throng laughed. Easy crowd. I pressed on. 'Of course, each and every one of you here tonight has helped us enormously over the past twelve months, whether that be through media coverage or engaging our services or . . .'

I spied Diane leaving her gingerbread post.

'. . . offering us some bitter lessons in business etiquette,' I continued through clenched teeth.

The mass in front of me tittered nervously and Samantha Priest heckled from the back row, 'Play nice, Jazzy Lou!' but I was too distracted by Diane's skeletal frame gliding through the crowd like a wraith.

'So the Bees and I want to thank you all . . .'

Diane paused by Belle Single near the ice luge, leaning in to whisper something in her ear.

'. . . very, very much,' I went on.

Em's finger slid down the running order to the next point of business: gift bags.

I nodded to show this was where I was headed. 'We want to thank you,' I repeated, 'for your friendship.'

Having spoken to Belle, Diane continued slicing through the crowd.

'And for your support.'

Belle trailed in Diane's wake.

'And for sticking by us!' I practically shouted this last point into the microphone as I was forced to stand and watch Diane and Belle Single, by now arm in arm, separate from the pack of revellers on the rooftop and disappear into the bathroom together. No doubt to snort coke through the rolled-up contract they'd just signed.

I could feel all my confidence, all my excitement, all my jubilation from earlier in the evening trickling through my fingers like sand.

In front of me, the crowd of partygoers stood expectantly.

'And so,' I pushed on desperately, 'as a gesture of our appreciation and as a celebration of Queen Bee's success so far,' my Bees appeared at various points around the room bearing gift bags, 'we'd like to leave you each with a very special gift.'

The crowd hummed excitedly. The Bees began dishing out gift bags. And Diane and Belle emerged triumphantly from the ladies room, a rolled-up bundle of papers tucked neatly under Diane's arm: her contract with Belle Single.

I plunged the knife into the Queen Bee anniversary cake and the fondant icing cracked under the pressure of the blade; soon the words Queen Bee 1st Anniversary, The taste of sweet success had been cut up into a hundred edible squares. As I wiped bright pink icing from the blade, I contemplated Queen Bee's own situation on the razor-sharp knife edge between success and failure. That was what this industry was like, I thought bitterly: everyone wanted a piece of you. And if you weren't careful, they'd simply eat you alive.

Traipsing up and down the stairs from the terrace that night, the Bees and I lugged the candy-hued remnants of the evening's revelry back to the reality of the office below as the last of our guests dispersed. Blissfully unaware of our near-won but then crushingly lost account with Belle Single, the Bees were as high as the helium balloons they ferried downstairs. I, on the other hand, felt nothing but deflated.

As I emerged at the top of the narrow stairwell to fetch yet another armful of oversized, sugar-inspired statues, I bumped into a stunning blonde coming the other way.

'Oh, I'm so sorry,' I excused myself. Attractive blondes might be a dime a dozen in Sydney, but you never knew who you might be bumping into. 'I hope you've had a fab evening at Queen Bee?' I flashed her a winning smile.

The blonde grinned back. 'Sure have, thanks. Always happy to raise a glass to anyone who's making it in PR in this town. Especially if their name's not Diane Wilderstein.'

I stopped in my tracks.

Especially if their name's *not* Diane Wilderstein? This was a girl after my own heart.

'Mazel tov to that, my friend,' I replied enthusiastically. 'Have we met?'

The blonde thrust out her hand. 'Holly. Nice to meet you.'

'Likewise. Anyone not on Team Wilderstein is a friend of mine.'

Holly laughed. 'I was though. On Team Wilderstein. In fact I sat at your desk after you . . . *departed*.' She chose this last word carefully.

'Oh, so you're one of Diane's protégées?' I asked, my eyes narrowing.

'*Was*,' she corrected. 'I was a junior publicist for Diane until she sacked me last week.'

I tried to keep the smirk off my face. 'And what was your offence? Getting in Diane's way before her first coffee of the day?'

Holly laughed again. 'Something like that.'

When she laughed Holly looked strangely familiar, as though her face had appeared on more than a Wilderstein mugshot.

'But you didn't start at Wilderstein till after I'd left?' I checked. Holly nodded. 'Are you sure we've never met before?'

Holly smiled bashfully. 'No, no, we've never met. But you might have seen my face before because my boyfriend is Craig Patricks . . .' She trailed off, embarrassed.

'Oh, of course!' I slapped my forehead. 'You're Holly Oliver.' No wonder I recognised her face. Holly Oliver was the fiancée of one of Australia's most celebrated track athletes and was forever being photographed on the red carpet at Olympic fundraising events, her long blonde hair as glossy as the mags that lapped up her picture-perfect relationship. Holly smiled again sheepishly and I made a split-second decision. A split-second decision I would later come to regret. 'Say, where are you working now, Holly Oliver? Given you and Diane Wilderstein have parted ways, that is?'

Holly raised a perfectly arched eyebrow. 'Um, nowhere actually. I've only been looking for a few days, though.'

I didn't need to see a CV. Being sacked by Diane was qualification enough for me. 'Perfect,' I announced. 'How would you like to come and work for me as a publicist at Queen Bee?'

Holly looked shocked. Then thrilled. 'I'd love to!' she agreed immediately and I stuck out my hand to shake on it. Holly promised exactly the sort of WAG glamour we needed to raise the profile of our hive. And if hiring her would piss off Diane then that didn't hurt either. In fact, after the stunt Diane had pulled tonight, this was just the beginning of what she could expect from Queen Bee. My quest for PR success now had an added motive: it would be all the more satisfying if it stung Diane.

Part
TWO

Part

TWO

11

'OMFG. I've just had an Anna Wintour moment,' I exploded, bursting into Allpress Café and turning heads for all the wrong reasons.

'So does the devil *really* wear Prada?' Luke asked drolly, barely looking up from his Perez Hilton app.

Perez was Luke's lifeblood so he'd failed to witness my illegal U-turn and rock-star park out the front. Luke that is, not Perez. If Perez were hanging out in Rosebery he would surely have spotted my advanced driving manoeuvre, not to mention the fact I performed it while simultaneously shouting down the phone at the Wintour of my discontent.

'Yes,' I fumed to Luke. 'She wears faux fur-covered devil horns. So last season for Prada. And she keeps them concealed under all that wild-woman hair.'

At this, Luke deserted Perez. 'Wild-woman hair? Jazz, no! Not Lillian Richard?' Then, even more incredulously: 'Tell me you haven't fucked off Lillian Richard?'

I'd just fucked off Lillian Richard.

I slid into my seat and launched into a monologue of how, exactly, I'd come to piss off the editor of *Eve Pascal* magazine (and third in line to the Richard dynasty) just weeks after we'd been sipping pink champagne together and exchanging pleasantries on the rooftop at Queen Bee's anniversary party. Pleasantries, admittedly, that included Diane Wilderstein (which tends to contradict the very meaning of the word). But pleasantries nonetheless. And now I'd gone and aggravated Lillian, one of my greatest allies.

'You know how it was the *Eve Pascal* Awards for fashion and beauty last night?' I said to Luke. 'Well, Lisse Cosmetics – one of our clients – is spending quite the dollar with *Eve Pascal* at the moment. They're dropping serious coin on magazine advertising plus, so they want blood from *Eve Pascal*. Blood in the form of beauty accolades. But when the winners of the makeup categories were read out at last night's awards, Lisse didn't walk away with a single gong. In fact, L'Oréal, their main competitor, won everything.' I barely stopped to draw breath. 'So I received an irate phone call from Lisse at some ungodly hour this morning, ranting and raving about *Eve Pascal* and where their gong belongs.'

'Ouch,' put in Luke.

'Ouch,' I agreed. 'Obviously, I told Lisse it was disappointing they didn't win an award. And, as their PR adviser, I asked them to consider mixing things up a little. Currently, they have all their eggs in one advertising basket with Commonwealth Combined

Print.' CCP is owned by the Richard dynasty. 'That's a lot of faith in one media group. Why not consider using some of CCP's competitors as well? Have themselves a little advertising omelette for brekkie, I suggested. I was only trying to be diplomatic. End of conversation. Next thing I know I've got Lillian Richard – who's transformed into the Anna Wintour of Sydney – on the phone going berserk!'

'No!'

'True story. And do you know what she said? She told me she was angry and disappointed with my advice about omelettes. Is this woman for real? "Angry"? "Disappointed"? I felt like I was in the principal's office being reprimanded! Shit, I'm lucky she didn't send me for detention. Is this seriously how she talks to people? No wonder she and Diane dine together.'

'Defs.' Luke nodded sagely.

'I'm not here to ruffle feathers,' I said.

'Just to scramble eggs,' Luke added.

'I can't help it if my clients get a taste for soufflé,' I shot back. 'At Queen Bee PR, we serve nothing less.'

'And what did Lillian think of your menu suggestions?' he asked.

Clunk. I slammed my hand down onto the table, bouncing Extra sachets everywhere. 'It seems she doesn't have the stomach for omelette. So now we can say *au revoir* to any press in *Eve Pascal*.'

'Unbelievable,' Luke mused. 'Now, what are we going to eat?'

Rolling my eyes at his dedication to his stomach despite my run-in with Richard III, I turned my attention to the menu. 'Wagyu beef burger? Club sandwich? You know I would never normally eat like this,' I said.

'Live a little,' was the response as he flagged down a waitress and ordered two Wagyu burgers with the lot. 'You can have a skinny mocha for lunch another day. Besides, it's not any old day you get to dine with the Sun's gossip columnist. I'm your bread and butter. You should be keeping me sweet, sweets.'

I popped four Nurofen with a swig of Santa Vittoria. 'Fine,' I said, offering my most saccharine smile. 'What if I get you an invite to the afterparty afterparty for the Coco Man of the Year Awards?'

Luke didn't need to be asked twice. A roomful of Australia's hottest men? And all of them bachelors? Better dust off his Dictaphone. 'Really?' he squealed, causing heads to swivel again. 'Fuck off! Jazz, you're the best!'

'And a plus-one for Reuben?' I asked, anticipating another squeal.

Luke frowned.

'No, Jefferson!' I exclaimed. 'Don't tell me it's over between you and Reuben?'

'Not over,' Luke replied, choosing his words carefully.

'But going under?' I suggested.

Luke nodded but offered no more.

'You okay?' I asked gently.

He nodded again. Clearly he was not ready to talk about it just yet.

'Good, because we've got work to do.' I changed the subject as our burgers arrived. 'I need to pick your brain about the

130

seating arrangements for the awards. It's a sit-down dinner for four hundred. Think glitz, glam, OTT. Très Sydney. We don't need to worry about catering or anything that crass. Just where guests will sit to eat said catering.'

'Black tie?' asked Luke, perking up.

'Naturally, babe,' I replied.

'Well,' he launched in, 'you can't invite a certain music reporter or their celeb companion. Did you see them steal two seats from the gossip journos at last week's do at the Wentworth? Really, if you're going to steal a seat don't steal it from someone who'll write nasty things about you.'

I pulled up the early stages of a spreadsheet on my iPad.

'And make sure you keep a particular style editor away from the action. And from any potential clients. Word on the street is she received a mystery package of Harmony PMS pills yesterday. Source unknown. And you don't get presents like that for playing nice.' Luke looked smug with this skerrick of goss.

'I heard.' I nodded, drumming my nails on the table. 'I'm spreading the word I'd like a delivery of Xanax, please.'

'Awesome,' retorted Luke. 'Save you yet another trip to your local chemist.' This was below the belt, as Luke knew perfectly well that I was under surveillance at my local pharmacy for my enthusiastic purchasing of Nurofen Plus. Honestly, what did they think I was going to do with five multipacks? Manufacture party drugs for anorexics? Twenty-five thousand milligrams wasn't going to get anyone over thirty-five kilograms excited. And as much as we'd all like to think otherwise, there wasn't anyone in my office fitting that description.

'Bitch,' I laughed. 'But have you heard about the other delivery going around this week? Paparazzi shots are being pumped out of a certain top-level model pashing a fashion designer. They're so staged you expect to see the model's management logo at the bottom of the attachment. No self-respecting journo is going to touch those images with a ten-foot pole.'

'Touché,' Luke said. 'That trumps a Samantha Priest paparazzi tip-off anyday.' I laughed again as I remembered how Samantha Priest, desperate to prop up her ailing profile, had visited Queen Bee HQ recently to raid our clothing samples. While leading Samantha through the showroom, I asked one of the Bees if the paps were outside, which everyone in the biz knows is code for: 'Call the paps and make sure they're outside.' The girls duly called Luke and he sent a photographer over to make Samantha feel loved as she left the building. I still owed him for that one.

'Beautiful – done,' I said, slipping my iPad into my Céline handbag, my head already back at the office. 'I'll get this,' I offered, making my way to the front counter.

'Next one's on me, babe,' Luke shouted after me.

'Perfect, let's eat at Otto,' I replied on my way out the door before jumping into my oh-so-handily-parked Range Rover. On the way back to the office I resisted the urge to check my voicemails, my emails and the latest tweets and blogs from the Bees, giving myself five minutes of uncontactable bliss. These precious few moments in the car are the only moments of silence in my day. Which is why I chose a teeny-tiny Aston Martin as my second car: there's no room for passengers.

Back at the office, I could hear the buzz of Bees even before I was through the front door. A buzz that would die suddenly, no doubt, when my YSLs were heard clicking up the stairs. It's not that I'm a ruthless boss. I worked for Diane long enough to know homicidal is not my style, and I'd be horrified to think any of the Bees was as miserable working for me as I was working for Diane. But I do think the cult of Cutrone has a point. Kelly Cutrone, that is, self-styled PR guru from the hit US TV show *Kell on Earth*, and author of *If You Have to Cry, Go Outside*. With her no-bullshit approach to work, I swear that woman is an inspiration. Still, I'd never send any of the Bees outside to cry. We don't have time to cry. And just think of the paps that could be out there . . .

Sure enough, as the sound of my red-soled stilettos pierced the air, the noise inside – a noise only a posse of Gen Y girls could make – suddenly muted. I buzzed myself in and stalked through the reception area. On my way to my desk, I paused by one of the clothing rails to inspect the media call-out sheet taped to the end of the rail. For Beautiful Bride *mag*, it read. *Dresses under $1500*. The rail was only half full yet the press call was marked urgent.

'Why hasn't this drop gone to *Beautiful Bride* magazine yet?' I boomed, my voice bouncing off the exposed cement walls. 'Alice, draft up an email to the editor explaining and I'll check it now. And someone get on to a courier, pronto,' I screeched. Honestly, we did two courier runs per day *each* in this office. You'd have thought they'd have the hang of it by now.

'Also, Lulu, can you get Leila Graham from Coco mag on the phone? We've made real progress with the seating for the Man of the Year Awards,' I continued, ricocheting round the office as I dished out directives.

'Alice, can you pick up all of Troy's accounts from now on?' I called, referring to our first (and probably last) male Bee, who I'd hired shortly after Holly.

'Yes,' Alice replied immediately. 'Only, where's Troy?'

'I fired him this morning,' I replied, flicking on my two computer screens.

'But you haven't been in the office yet today!' she gasped incredulously.

'Keep up, Alice. Haven't you heard of SMS? And let that be a warning to any of you who thinks two lunch breaks and then a spray tan is a good way to spend the afternoon when I'm out of the office.

'Anya, your blog about the new Elle Macpherson Intimates range is totally lustworthy,' I called, having read it on my way in from the car. 'And Emma, what time am I due at Schwarzkopf?'

Telltale white iPod ear buds disappeared into desk drawers and Facebook slid off screens around the office. The boss was back.

Seated at my desk, in front of my two computer screens, I made mental lists of what we needed to achieve with the rest of the afternoon. And then I made lists of my lists. We still hadn't heard back from HOTMilk Maternity Lingerie after our pitch, so drastic action was needed. Cupcakes. Surely someone over at HOTMilk was pregnant and had given up all hope of fitting into this season's Hervé Léger? Cupcakes would go down a treat and it was touches like these that won accounts.

'Emma, can you give Sparkle Cupcakery a buzz and order a box for HOTMilk?' I called across to her. 'Something warm and fuzzy in pinks and blues, please. But cakes with a bit of bite too, yeah? This is HOTMilk, not warm cocoa.'

Emma nodded and picked up her phone. We sent more than a hundred boxes of cupcakes a month to sweeten clients and industry contacts, so Emma had Sparkle on speed dial. I swear we financed Sparkle's famous fundraising for schools program singlehandedly. There were kids in primary schools all across Sydney wiping crumbs from their mouths and years from their lives through obesity and heart disease and they only had us to thank. Better not point that out to the yummy-mummies-to-be over at HOTMilk.

Of course, all of this was just icing on the cake compared with our major project for the year (and what I hoped would be the crème de la crème of my career to date now that Belle Single and *Kitchen Divas* was off the menu): BMW Australian Fashion Week. The jewel of the Emerald City's fashion calendar, BMW Australian Fashion Week was a much-anticipated fixture among fashionistas. And this year's event was our chance to cut it in the big time. You see, our darling client, designer Allison Palmer, was showing her latest shimmering collection at Fashion Week and we Bees would leave no sequin unturned to ensure her show — and the future of Queen Bee — was a success. When added to the *Coco Man of the Year Awards*, I was hopeful we'd see out the year in style. But first we had a diabolical amount of work to do.

'Oh, and Em?' I remembered. 'Could you grab a thousand dollars from my account this afternoon when you're out at the post office, please, hon?' Emma does all my ATM transactions for me. Without her, there'd never be a note in my wallet.

'Sure, love,' came the reply. 'But more cash? Do you have plans for this evening, Jazz?'

Cheeky bitch. The only problem with having your right-hand girl run your diary for you is that your right-hand girl knows when you've got a date. Not that my love life (or lack thereof) was any secret in this office. Everyone knew that, since I dated Will, my relationships seemed to disappear faster than you could say *Underbelly*. And while in the gangland miniseries most everyone died as a result of the mob whereas in my love life things usually died out as a result of my *job*, the number of corpses left strewn around was remarkably similar.

'Sure I have plans,' I replied coyly to Emma. 'Anya and I are having drinks with the star of the new Converse ad campaign, the Canadian singer Tom Reynolds. Oh, and Ben Gorman from Converse will be there too.' I tried not to look too smug at the mention of Ben.

Emma snorted. 'Ben Gorman. Head of Sales for Converse shoes? I should have guessed. It wouldn't be a romantic evening out unless it was work-related in some way, would it, Jazzy Lou?'

Ben Gorman was dreamy and designer-label-conscious and directly connected to my working life in a way that was potentially disastrous if things didn't work out between us romantically, and that ticked all my boyfriend-requirement boxes if it did.

Em went on, 'You do realise that an after-work meeting with Ben Gorman to align your sales and publicity strategies does not actually constitute a date?'

I raised one I'm-still-your-boss-remember? eyebrow. 'Sure,' I said. 'But how many people discuss strategic alignment while in the presence of crooner Tom Reynolds, the fantasy of bored housewives the world over, huh?' The guy oozed romance from every pore. Just having him there for our discussions meant there'd be more hearts involved than a Dotti range, surely.

Em was clearly not convinced but had enough sense not to say so.

'Plus,' I added, 'if things don't work out romantically between Ben and me, at the very least I can fill him in on what we've got planned for the opening of Converse's new Melbourne store. The launch there is going to be *amaze*. At least, it will be if I ever hear back from the Melbourne office with sign-off on the final press list . . .' I checked my phone compulsively.

'Great,' Em said. 'So once you've had your highly romantic – but no doubt productive – conversation about strategy in the Asia Pacific, what else will you and Ben Gorman from Sales align, Jazz?'

'I'm afraid that's strictly confidential,' I grinned.

Just then my phone *did* ring, interrupting my daydream of strategic collaboration with Ben Gorman's range. 'It's Amanda from Coast Underwear for you,' Lulu said down the line from reception.

Fuck.

'Okay, thanks, Lulu,' I said. 'Put her through.'

'Jasmine! Hello!' Amanda gushed, her voice dripping with insincerity. 'I can't believe I caught you in the office. I thought you'd be out at some fabulous media launch.' At four-thirty on a Wednesday afternoon? Really? Did this girl actually work in PR? 'I expected to get one of your minions, not you,' she added.

My minions? We might be called Queen Bee but I'm no Duchess. I spent a moment fantasising about what the Bees would do to Amanda if they heard themselves referred to as minions. Being paraded down George Street in last season's Chanel wouldn't be punishment enough.

'Oh well, Amanda, you know me,' I said lightly. 'I like to be here on the front line for my clients. Otherwise it'd be like being a designer and not designing the new range. We've got a signature here at Queen Bee PR and people come to me for that signature look so I really need to be here when they call.'

Was that a sneer coming down the line? Amanda and I had a difficult working relationship. She was the kind of publicist who made Lizzie Grubman look like Mother Teresa.

'I'm glad you called, Amanda,' I lied. 'We need to nut out the scope of Coast Underwear's involvement in the Coco Man of the Year Awards campaign. As a major sponsor, does Coast want a presence at the media call announcing the winners? And at any publicity shoots before then? And I'll need some merch to kick off the campaign, please.'

This was Amanda's cue to say, 'Sure, a dozen boxes of product will be couriered to QB HQ this afternoon.' If only.

'Oh, before we start talking product, Jasmine, I'm afraid I'll have to run you through the Coast protocol first.'

She was shitting me, surely? 'Fine, shoot,' I replied. I could hear a smattering of typing on the other end of the line and wondered what sort of manifesto Amanda was bringing up on her screen.

'First, and most importantly, under no circumstances must Coast models ever be naked.'

At this I cracked up and wondered – for the first time – whether Amanda and I might actually be able to get on for the duration of this campaign after all. I'd clearly underestimated her sense of humour.

Or not.

'Er, you know they're male underwear models, right, Amanda?'

Silence.

'It's not like they're unfamiliar with flashing their bits, yeah?'

Nothing.

'Okay, well, let's clarify exactly what you mean by naked then,' I tried, realising we weren't going to get far like this. 'Can the models go topless?'

'I guess.'

'Underwear only?'

'It's Coast policy to have all models wearing trousers of some kind. Even if they're photographed in the process of removal.'

'Short shorts?'

'Cargos.'

'A towel?'

'Bathsheet size. Not standard.'

'What about bare feet?' I was getting exasperated.

'I'll check.'

'Great,' I said. 'You check whether your models can appear sans sandals, and I'll order twenty XXL bathsheet-sized beach towels to go.'

'Fine,' she said, and hung up.

Luckily Em chose this moment to appear beside my desk with a skim mocha and ten crisp one-hundred-dollar bills from my account.

'I've just discovered our Coast underwear models are more Mormon than showmen,' I said to her. 'I'm surprised Amanda lets them out without a chastity belt.'

Em raised one Parlour B-manicured eyebrow quizzically but knew better than to ask further questions. Stranger things happened in this office every day.

'And thanks for the coffee and funds,' I added. 'You're a lifesaver, love.'

My mobile buzzed on my desk and I steeled myself for round two with Amanda. I checked the screen through wincing eyes, expecting the worst. *Shelley*, it read.

'Thank God!' I answered. 'At least you won't try to convert me to Mormonism.'

'Sweetie,' she drawled, not missing a beat, 'why do you need God when you've got me? You won't believe what I've just bought. The most amaze Rodarte caramel silk-tulle dress in wood-print silk. Never mind the Mormons, this is divine! You have to have it.'

I laughed and thanked God for the breath of fresh air Shelley always brought to my working day. 'It sounds amazing, Shell,' I said. 'But why don't −'

'It is,' she cut me off at the pass. 'It's got a hand-embroidered bodice, all chocolate and caramels, and a tulip skirt. It will look incred with that gold Anya Hindmarch clutch I gave you last month.'

'That sounds good enough to eat, hon,' I said. 'But why don't you keep it? I can always borrow it from you sometime.'

But Shell was having none of it. 'Pleeease. We've been through this whole borrowing thing before. It's a gift. I want you to have it. Besides,' she added, 'turns out Rodarte looks bigger on Net-a-Porter's website than it does in a black box in your living room. I can barely get one arm into this dress, so you'll have to take it from me.'

Officer, how could I resist an offer like that? Slap on the handcuffs, I was guilty as charged.

'I'd love to!' I said to Shell. 'In fact, I've got a *date* tonight.' I looked pointedly at Em who was within earshot. 'And it sounds like the perfect outfit for an evening of seduction.' I said this last sentence loud enough to be heard in the outskirts of greater metropolitan Sydney.

'It *is*, dah-ling,' she assured me. 'Even you can get laid in Rodarte.'

'Really?' I asked, glad greater metropolitan Sydney hadn't caught that one. 'Even I can get laid in Rodarte? Did it say that in the Editor's Notes on Net-a-Porter, Shell?'

Shelley laughed. 'Just come by before eight to pick it up, love.'

12

Tom Reynolds, Canadian crooner and the face of Converse, didn't need to be my Facebook friend for me to work out his status.

'Jock,' I said to Anya as we sat in the wine bar at Felix waiting for Ben and his charge to arrive. I shifted on my bar stool and the caramel silk skirt of my new Rodarte dress slid luxuriously over my skin. 'His passport might say Canuck but I bet my Miu Miu store card this guy's more all-American jock than his Calvin Klein undies.'

'CK boxers?' Anya said dreamily.

'More like briefs. Real brief. Blink and you miss it kinda stuff, I reckon. Anyone who can hold a note for that long must be lacking in stamina somewhere else.'

Anya ignored me. She was too busy looking past me so she could spy Mr Reynolds the instant he appeared. Her strength as a publicist might have been growing every day but her weakness for celebrities was unchanged. I nearly feared for Tom Reynolds this evening. It didn't matter who he was or what direction his star was headed, the very fact he was famous made him fair game in Anya's eyes.

'Sorry we're late, ladies,' Ben said moments later, sauntering up to the pewter bar with real Parisian subway tiles on the walls. He was wearing a fitted charcoal Hugo Boss suit, all narrow lapels and stovepipe trousers, tapered just so at the ankles. A skinny black tie completed the just-from-the-office look. My favourite.

He had Tom Reynolds in tow.

'All my fault, I'm afraid,' added Tom, his long vowels dripping with charm. 'Call me irresponsible,' he added, shaking Anya's hand.

'Hello, Irresponsible,' Anya swooned.

Ben nudged me in amusement.

I swooned.

This was going to be a long night.

'So what do you ladies do for fun Down Under?' Tom asked, settling himself next to Anya at the bar and causing her to choke on her champagne.

'Yeah, what do you do for fun down under, Jazz?' Ben repeated suggestively, before ordering a couple of beers. 'Got any tips?' A smile curled at the corners of his take-me-now Gregory Peck mouth.

'Well, it depends what turns you on, Tom,' I said, forcing myself to turn away from Ben. 'If slow and indulgent is your thing, you could try Endota Spa at Martin Place. Or, if you prefer it fast and furious, there's always Derby Day at the Spring Racing Carnival.'

Ben grinned and raised his glass almost imperceptibly. That smile again. It was enough to make a girl gloss over the fact Endota and Derby Day were both clients and what he thought was cheesy flirting was just a shameless plug.

'Wow,' said Tom, turning back to Anya. 'Do you fancy either of those?'

'Sure, quando, quando, quando?' Anya said coyly, struggling not to fall off her bar stool.

Several hours (and more than several drinks) later, the evening had alcohol on its breath. Much as I would never grow tired of Ben's bar-side banter, I reluctantly realised it was time to bail. I had a final planning meeting for the Coco Man of the Year Awards' press campaign tomorrow, and more than a little work to do before then.

'Time is money, peeps,' I said. 'I should be getting back to the office.'

Ben looked shocked. Anya just looked wasted.

'Are you for real? You're going back to work now? Who does overtime at this hour?' Ben said churlishly.

I hesitated. I wasn't sure I liked the edge that had just crept into his voice; it was more than vaguely reminiscent of the tone Will used to take whenever we discussed my workaholism. But, with several champagnes under my Hermès belt and a rapidly increasing crush to boot, my judgement was cloudy. Best just to chalk it up to Ben being bereft at the thought of me bailing.

'No one's leaving,' interrupted our international superstar. 'Because you ladies are coming back to my penthouse for a nightcap!' He added a wink for good measure.

'Killer!' Anya said.

'Kill me,' I said, but low enough for only Ben to hear. I added to Ben, 'If I go you go . . .'

He rewarded me with that Gregory Peck grin and reached into his jacket pocket for his wallet.

'No, no. I'll get this,' I insisted. 'It's a Queen Bee treat.' I went to retrieve the cash Em had slipped me earlier, only to find my wallet bare.

'Shit. Where's my money gone?' I wondered aloud as Tom Reynolds was already staggering for the exit, weighed down with a very drunk Anya. 'And where the hell's Anya going?' I slapped my black Amex on the bar and turned to Ben. 'We have to look after her.'

'Whatever it takes?' Ben asked, quoting from a Reynolds hit.

'Whatever it takes.' I volleyed seductiveness back at his suggestiveness and we headed for the door in hot pursuit of Anya, who was all over Tom Reynolds like a rash. If fame was indeed like a sexually transmitted disease, then someone needed to vaccinate that girl. And quick.

In no time at all, Anya, Ben and I found ourselves in the penthouse apartment of the nearby exclusive Ivy hotel for our own private Tom Reynolds concert. It was hard to believe the last time I'd been inside this sprawling suite, all dark wood and marble and overlooking the Ivy's famous rooftop pool, was for Raven's photo shoot with *Look*. How things had changed. While the Ivy, like a fine wine, was ageing gracefully, Raven had proved more of a fizzer. Last I'd heard she'd been dumped as the face of Vixenary after a series of illegal but unsurprising drug-related indiscretions. Plus her singing career was finally sunk.

If only the same could be said for Mr Reynolds.

'Fly me to the moon . . .' he crooned from behind his baby grand as Anya draped herself precariously across the piano lid to be closer to her dream date. I preferred the U-shaped leather couches myself. Plenty of room there for me to cosy up to Ben.

'Benny, why don't you get us all a little something to drink?' our pianist sang, raising one hand from the keys just long enough to gesture towards the bar in an adjoining room. Benny was duly dispatched and my plans for canoodling dismissed.

'And Jazzy Lou, hit the lights! We need a little atmosphere in here, baby,' Tom directed me during the bridge. Seriously, this was like being on stage with the Jersey Boys. I left Liberace and his adoring fan to it in the sunken lounge and under the pretence of looking for the lighting remote went off exploring the rest of the recently revamped pad.

'This place has everything!' I exclaimed when I found Ben in the marble bar where he was concocting drinks.

'Totes,' he agreed. 'Although I'm not sure I want to know why any hotel room needs eight showerheads in the bathroom.'

'For real?' I laughed, leaning against him for just long enough to scoop up a cocktail, then I left to investigate the communal shower situation for myself.

'LOL! And a spa pool!' I called back over my shoulder as I wandered through the open-plan suite, dodging the sculptural light fittings on the way. Worth remembering for later in the night if things went well with Ben. Stopping off in the luxury bedroom, I sprawled out on the bed and breathed in the three-hundred-thread-count pillowcases. Watching my reflection in all that marble, I sipped my lychee and passionfruit caprioska, the saccharine syrup sweetening my Tom Reynolds experience. This wasn't so bad. I could put up with a little celebrity fawning by Anya if it gave me an excuse to spend more time basking in Ben's beguiling company. And, hell, even the Broadway serenade from the lounge room had stopped.

Shit. The Broadway serenade from the lounge room had stopped. This couldn't be good.

Skidding across the marble floor, slopping fruit-infused alcohol as I went, I got back to the lounge just in time to see Tom abandon his instrument with a violent crash of keys. Anya, who was passed out against the ebony lid, woke and yelped.

'Sorry, babe. It's just too bright in here,' Tom said by way of explanation, then kissed her seductively on the neck. Anya creamed herself quietly while our host stalked out of the room and then re-emerged dragging a suitcase behind him.

'Shades!' he exclaimed in his best Broadway voice. As if that explained anything.

I propped Anya upright.

'Shades!' he repeated louder, ringmaster style, before opening his suitcase to reveal hundreds of pairs of Ray-Ban sunglasses, in every colour, shape and design, stacked neatly in row upon

UV-fighting row. Holy shit. This guy was the Imelda Marcos of eyewear. He could fit out every Stevie Wonder impersonator in the southern hemisphere with this stash and still have leftovers. Hell, you'd probably never have to see daylight again with that collection.

Reynolds slipped on a pair of shiny aviators, turning his head from side to side as if sizing up his choice, before turning to me and Anya. 'Ladies, be my guest,' he invited suggestively, then gestured belatedly to the sunnies.

Anya giggled from where I finally had her upright on the piano seat.

'Eye care is no laughing matter, baby,' he deadpanned, before brushing a strand of rogue GHD'd hair behind her ear as he sat back down beside her at the instrument.

'Fly me to the moon . . .' he began yet again and Anya joined in the singing this time. At least she could be confident of the words. We'd heard them ten fucking times already.

At this point Ben returned with our drinks and interrupted our Ray Charles convention. 'What the . . . ? Why the hell are you all wearing sunglasses?' he asked.

I flashed Ben my best everyone-else-here-is-crazy smile before patting the space on the lounge beside me.

He returned my grin, plonking a bottle of whisky on the piano lid and another drink in Anya's hand, before joining me on the couch where he chivalrously topped up my glass.

'Wayfarer or Wings?' I said to him dryly, offering up two pairs of sunnies.

Ben slid closer, ignoring my question and pushing the sunnies out of the way before slipping his hand along my leg. 'Bet you weren't expecting this tonight?' he asked, probably referring to the zaniness that engulfed us from every corner of the room. But I couldn't think beyond his hand. *Yes!* I wanted to shout. *Yes, this I was hoping for!*

'No,' I replied instead, struggling to talk and breathe at the same time as Ben's hand made its way up my thigh. And then: 'I thought we'd at least cover off your sales plan for the new range.' Shit, what did I go and say that for? The truth was, it had been a while and, much as I wanted Ben – had been wanting him all evening – now the opportunity was here I was surprising even myself by stalling.

'Sales plan?' Ben gave me the same look Emma had just hours earlier. 'But this beats going back to the office like you were planning, right?' His hand moved higher and he kissed me lightly on my exposed shoulder as if to distract me.

In the corner, Anya and Tom were busily undressing one another, Tom fumbling to unhook her bra with one hand while still tickling the ivories with his other. This was hardly the romantic rendezvous I had hoped of for Ben and me.

'Let's move to another room,' I said, hoping for seductive and not just instructive. I know most guys like a woman who takes charge but I am also aware that I don't really need to amp up this side of my personality. Giving orders comes especially easy to me.

Ben looked pleased. 'Now that's more like it,' he added before planting those Gregory Peck lips on mine.

As we stood to seek out some five-star privacy, with Ben's arm wrapped agreeably around my waist, my handbag on the couch began to vibrate urgently. For the briefest of seconds I hesitated.

Then my phone started to ring proper.

I paused. Ben looked at me questioningly. I returned his gaze. Then glanced at my ringing phone. Then back at Ben.

It was late. The only person ringing me now had to be calling from the Converse Hong Kong office. I *needed* to take this call.

'It's Converse in Honkers,' I began, as if to appeal to the business branch of his brain.

Ben's eyes narrowed as he dragged them back from the bedroom where they'd been heading.

'It's got to be about the new store launch —' I tried again.

Ben's hand gripped my waist. I could feel him leaning towards the bedroom.

The phone continued to ring.

I stood fixed to the spot, torn between the threat of letting the long-awaited call go to voicemail and letting go of the male standing beside me.

'Jazz . . .' said Ben, leaning in to kiss me.

The phone wouldn't ring much longer. Voicemail *had* to be about to kick in. Only my business sense kicked in first.

Holding Ben back with one arm, I bent down and reefed my ringing phone from my clutch with the other.

'Hello, Jasmine Lewis,' I rushed down the line.

'Jasmine? Sasha here from the Hong Kong office . . .'

Got it in time. I breathed a sigh of relief. Ben, on the other hand, wasn't so pleased. He ripped his arm away from my waist and stormed over to the piano to pour himself another whisky, clearly sore at losing out to my BlackBerry.

Moments later, my conversation with Hong Kong all wrapped up, I ventured over to Ben to make it up to him. Only he didn't give me a chance.

'Do you come with an off switch, Jazzy Lou?' he asked, heading back to the couch I'd just come from and forcing me to trail behind him.

'Hell no,' I said proudly.

The look on his face told me this was not the answer he was hoping for. I was beginning to feel as welcome as a tweet at the Logies.

In the corner Tom Reynolds was persisting in his wooing of Anya. 'Fly me to the – I know what we need!' he warbled, disappearing momentarily to rummage around in the bar.

I turned to Ben. 'Okay, this might be my cue to split. Much as I don't want to leave Anya, it's getting a little bit *Alice in Wonderland* in here and I'm late for a very important date with some sleep if I want to get up and work tomorrow.' The sparkle of the suite that had so impressed me barely an hour ago was beginning to fade. Fast. What hurt a little was that Ben put up no argument.

'Fine.' He shrugged.

Our host, however, chose that moment to return, inspiration in hand. 'Apple bong!' he announced triumphantly, holding a Granny Smith unsteadily in the air with a baseball mitt, before returning to his piano stool.

'Fly me to the moon . . .'

Here we go again.

'Ooh, what's that?' Anya was now conscious. But barely.

'This baby,' said Reynolds, throwing the apple up in the air and catching it in his mitt while still playing the piano dexterously with the other hand, 'is one fucking Granny Smith apple stuffed with the finest quality grass this side of Kingston Town.'

Anya snuggled up closer.

'Fly me to the moon . . .' came the familiar refrain, getting faster and faster each time, like some dizzying merry-go-round that just wouldn't stop.

The air that had soured between me and Ben was now filled with the acrid scent of marijuana as our host sparked up. Here on the couch, however, sparks of an entirely different kind were beginning to fly as Ben had clearly decided not to go down without a fight.

'What's the deal, Jazz?' he asked accusingly. 'You act like you're all interested and then, when faced with missing just one fucking phone call, you switch from the bedroom back to the boardroom in the blink of an eye.'

I grimaced apologetically. 'I'm sor—' I began, ready to explain that it *was* his account that I had been looking after, but – ego clearly bruised – Ben was having none of it.

'You're all batting eyelashes one minute then business plans the next. I can't be arsed with that.'

In the corner the apple bong was being thrown up and down and up and down, despite the fact it was lit. Just what I needed. An insurance bill from Merivale when the Canuck burned the place down.

I turned to Ben. 'Chill. It was just one phone call,' I said.

Up and down and up and down. The apple continued to soar through the air, miraculously landing with a dull thud back into the baseball mitt each time. The room was spinning and I couldn't tell if it was the incessant music or all those caprioskas I'd been downing, but one thing was for sure: Anya was being flown to the moon over there in the corner.

'One phone call,' Ben mimicked, bringing me back down to earth. 'At exactly the moment I thought we were getting somewhere. I didn't hang around all night to watch you be a switchboard bitch.'

Up and down and up and down. That apple just won't stop.

I stared into my cocktail glass, willing myself to keep calm. Ben was totally overreacting. It was just one stupid work call. I couldn't afford to lose my cool — or the Converse account — just because Ben was being a douche.

But why wouldn't the damn music ever end?

My phone buzzed again: *Has the Rodarte worked its magic yet, babe?* Shelley texted.

I hit delete.

'You know you're more impossible princess than queen bee,' Ben goaded me again.

I bit my tongue. *You've got to work with this guy, you've got to work with this guy,* I repeated over and over in my head. All thoughts of romance were now well and truly banished. Having seen Ben's temper, I was suddenly not keen on seeing anything else he wanted to reveal tonight.

Up and down and up and down.

Anya was now sitting on Reynolds' lap with her tongue down his throat and the piano was still playing the same damned refrain.

'Am I wrong?' Ben tried again. 'Tell me I'm wrong, Jazzy Lou.'

Oh God, someone flip the record.

Up and down and up and down. Why wouldn't the spinning stop?

And then the crash of shattering glass splintered the air and the spinning room came immediately to a halt. A half-full bottle of Kentucky whisky lay in a million pieces on the floor and golden liquid seeped away in all directions while Anya looked up in sleepy surprise, as if unable to connect her and Reynolds' grabbing arms with the smashed bottle at her feet.

'I think that's our cue to exit stage left, babe,' our star drawled drunkenly, before dragging Anya off in the direction of the sprawling bedroom. I raised my eyebrows at Anya on her way past but she flashed me a victorious smile and so I merely watched her go.

'Well, now, haven't you got a spreadsheet or a media list to update?' Ben asked me, slurring ever so slightly. That last, fast glass of whisky had clearly kicked in. 'I'd hate to get between you and your profit margin. Surely there's some overtime you could be doing?'

Finally, this was too much. I felt fury rise in my throat. Sure, I'd chosen business over pleasure, electing not to drag Ben off to bed at the very moment it looked like I would. And sure, I'd taken a work call when he was trying to work me in other ways. But that didn't mean we couldn't have continued once I'd hung up. If only he hadn't been such a dick about it all.

For a minute, silence hung over the room as we sat sans serenade. Then slowly, deliberately, as if watching myself moving in slow motion, I reached for my cocktail glass, lifted it as if to my mouth and then changed direction at the last minute and instead poured the entire sticky contents all over Ben's crotch.

'Faaaark!' Ben swore. 'What the hell did you do that for?' Getting up, he stormed into the bar for towels.

I sat and contemplated my empty glass. *Well, Jazzy Lou, you may have finally done it this time,* I thought. *No man cops a caprioska to the crotch and takes it lying down.*

And yet I can't say I was entirely sorry. Even though the Converse account would surely walk out the door, even though my fling with Ben was over before it had begun, I'd do the same all over again. Because dismissing someone's profit margin just ain't funny.

I felt my fury rise again. 'You know what your problem is, Ben Gorman?' I shouted after him, summoning the very worst insult I could think of. 'Your problem is you don't appreciate the value of doing a little overtime.'

And with that I stalked out of the room.

I was jerked awake from a groggy, drunken sleep the next morning by the sound of my BlackBerry ringing. Throwing an arm out wildly, I knocked my copy of *Nice Girls Just Don't Get It* from the bedside table before laying my hand on the phone.

'Jasmine Lewis, hello?' I managed, hauling myself awake.

'Jazz?' a voice whispered down the line.

WTF?

'Jazz, it's Anya,' whispered the voice again.

'Anya?' I repeated, slowly coming around. 'Sorry, I didn't recognise you without your theme music. Where the hell are you, babe?'

'I'm still at the Ivy,' Anya whispered and then I heard that all-too-familiar warble somewhere in the background.

'You're still at the Ivy?' I choked.

'Uh, yeah. Tommy's in the shower,' she added unnecessarily. 'Um, Jazz, what do I do now?'

OMG. 'Do you think he's waiting to invite you to breakfast?' I asked incredulously. 'PR 101, love: don't sleep with the client. But if you fail that course, here's what they'll teach you at summer school: don't hang around in the morning!'

'Er, right,' Anya said, sounding simultaneously disappointed and relieved at being given an out.

'Get out of there now, babe! And Anya?'

'Yeah?'

'Down with love,' I declared, raiding Reynolds' back catalogue one last time before hanging up.

Later that morning, Shelley popped up in my inbox with the postcoital post-mortem I knew was coming my way:

From: Shelley Shapiro
Title: Best friend
Time: 10.23 am

Dah-ling? Where are you? Still lying in bed somewhere, I hope . . . S x

PS Did that Rodarte number pinch around the neck?

Popping a bunch of Nurofen to erase the final traces of last night, I smiled ruefully at Shelley's message. I wasn't sure what surprised me less, Shell's unswerving faith in my love life or her complete inability to grasp the concept of a working week. Did she really think I might be sprawled out on a Sealy Posturepedic somewhere, my sexual conquest feeding me grapes and politely ignoring the fact it was 10.30 am on a weekday?

I tried not to dwell on the fact I'd been at my desk for over three hours already as I banged out a reply.

Hey Babe,

Um, I'd be lying if I said I was still lying in bed. In fact, I'd be lying if I said we ever made it there at all. Long story. Suffice to say, I thought Tom Reynolds would make for the perfect soundtrack to our romantic evening. Turns out The Kills would have been better. Don't think I'll be hearing from Ben again. But at least the Rodarte fits, right? And there's always the Coco Man of the Year Awards kicking off tomorrow to cheer me up. Nothing says 'I'm over him' like parading around town with twenty semi-naked men! JL xxx

13

Persuading twenty of Australia's hottest bachelors to take off their shirts and preen, pose and play up to the Sydney media should have been the easiest job in the world. My goodness, if you wander down to Bondi Park any day of the week, you'd have a hard time finding a guy with his shirt on. It's not our glistening harbour that earned Sydney its nickname the Emerald City. More like the sun's blinding rays bouncing off all those well-oiled, hairless metrosexuals standing round admiring themselves in their budgie-smugglers. So organising the PR for the Coco Man of the Year Awards should have been a walk in the, ahem, park. Right?

Wrong. So, so wrong.

Day one of the two-day Man of the Year Awards media juggernaut dawned wet and soggy, rather than hot and steamy like our guys. Still, us Bees weren't going to let a little tropical monsoon rain on our parade. First order of business was to issue the press release announcing the finalists. But this was not just *any* presser. This was a laminated media release, meticulously placed underneath a decadent one-kilogram 'bed' of chocolate cake, complete with icing sugar bedsheets discreetly covering our pièce de résistance: a (never-nude) miniature Coast model in the form of a doll. This was sure to win over the hearts and stomachs of newsrooms all across Sydney. As long as we could deliver them in one piece. And that's where things began to get tricky.

Launching myself through the doors at QB HQ I was greeted by an army of worker Bees, hair styled to perfection and stilettos sky high. Today was Coco Man of the Year day and these girls were taking no prisoners. The ever-reliable Em was leading the charge, ticking items off a checklist as I jumped into the fray and began shouting to be heard over the rain thundering on the roof.

'Alice, you and Anya will cover the magazines at CCP media group. I'll head there in a separate car too. Lulu, you and Holly look after the opposition at Media Central Magazines. And Lulu, did you double-triple-confirm with the Smart car delivery guy this morning? I've heard from Planet Cake that the cakes are on their way here now.'

On cue, a courier van beeped its horn out the front and I ran back out into the rain.

Despite the courier parking right out the front of our building, there was still a median strip, a footpath and a flight of outdoor stairs to be traversed in order to get twenty very delicate hand-crafted cakes safely into the building. And all during a flash flood. It was time to rally the troops.

'Okay, loves, your country needs you!' I announced, equipping each Bee with a Queen Bee-branded umbrella before grabbing one for myself and leading the way to the door. 'And be careful in those shoes,' I fussed before I could stop myself. Then added, 'I can't afford your workers' comp bill.' The last thing I needed was for someone to slip and break more than a heel. In fact, that's why I always carry my trusty Chanel flats in my handbag. Sure, stilettos are required for my look when I'm with clients but who can run in heels all day?

Braving the rain and sacrificing our blow-waves, we filed outside to form a conga line of cake couriers. As each shiny white box filled with a culinary work of art was gingerly passed along the line from one Bee to the next, the troops gradually emptied the back of the delivery van and filled our reception with sweet treats. It was enough to make any general proud.

But there's no rest for the wicked and no sooner had the cake delivery van left than a semitrailer carrying half-a-dozen Mercedes-Benz ForTwo Micro Hybrid Drives – or Smart cars – pulled up in its place. And now our day really started to get interesting. You see, Mercedes-Benz was the principle sponsor of the *Coco* awards. And as a key sponsor their Smart cars needed to have a huge presence at all things Man of the Year-related. So we needed to use Smart cars for every move we made. Having a media call? There should be a string of Mercedes Smart cars parked out the front of the venue. Driving a finalist to a press interview? Smart car it was. Delivering a press-release-slash-cake to all the major press outlets like we were this morning? You guessed it.

So my army of miniskirt-clad, stiletto-wearing, P-plate-wielding Bees and I were about to be let loose on six brand-spanking-new top-of-the-range Mercedes-Benz Smart cars in the rain. Weren't nothing smart about that. Our delivery guy clearly didn't think so either. His instructions were to have us drive the cars off the trailer ourselves, in reverse. But one look at me and the Bees and he decided he might do this for us. Smart man, that delivery guy.

'I bags the red one!' (Alice)

'OMG! Have you seen the stereo in here? It has a remote!' (Anya)

'Who needs a remote in a car the size of a matchbox?' (Em)

'Is there enough room for the cakes?' (Me)

'Why are there three pedals?' (Lulu)

'Lulu, have you ever driven a manual before?' (Holly, strapped into the passenger seat of Lulu's car)

'No. But I've seen my boyfriend drive one.' (Lulu)

'Check out the sunroof!' (Alice)

'I don't care if it's got airbags!' (Holly, no longer strapped into the passenger seat of Lulu's car)

Slowly, one by one, we manoeuvred the Smart cars out of the street and headed for our various delivery destinations. Parting ways at the end of Botany Road, we would all be meeting up at the Beresford Hotel in Surry Hills afterwards in order to prep the venue ahead of tomorrow's media briefing. In the meantime, we had cakes to deliver.

Swinging the car up onto the pavement at Martin Place, in the heart of Sydney's Calibre-clad corporate sector, I dodged a few lawyers with their trolley-toting lackeys and bunged on my hazard lights. Using hazards to park illegally might not be exactly lawful in the RTA's eyes but, believe me, for a roomful of *Wake Up!* TV staff who had been on set since three-thirty this morning, the delivery of a sugar hit qualified as an emergency.

I abandoned the car – doors open and lights flashing – and headed straight for Channel Six's main reception where Joe behind the front desk slipped me a visitor's pass and waved me on through. Making my way through the rabbit warren of corridors and staircases at Six, I finally found myself in the producers' suite, where they were planning tomorrow's episode.

'Cake delivery!' I called, lifting the lid on the white box in my arms and revealing my mini Coast model in all his glory. Well, almost all his glory. Let's not forget that strategically placed icing-sugar bedsheet covering his modesty (and my arse).

'Cake? Are you serious?' The exec producer, Bec, was first on her feet. 'Jasmine Lewis, you are my hero. Whatever you're spruiking, you can have the 8 am slot for it. Now come in here with that cake.'

And that, my friends, is how to get on TV. Skip the presenters and go straight for the engine room of production. Nothing you've ever seen when you switch on your flat screen has made it there without the approval of an executive producer somewhere. That television producers mainly live on a diet of coffee and deadlines is no revelation to cake-bearing PRs. Feeding sugar to producers is easier than taking candy from a baby.

I entered the room as people cleared a space on the boardroom table for me to place my sacrificial Coast cake. And that's when they noticed him. 'Check this out! There's a naked man on the cake!' someone called out.

'LOL!'

'Never nude,' I deadpanned, before launching into my pitch. 'Okay, *Wake Up!*, it's the *Coco* Man of the Year Awards again and, just for you, I can do a couple of nice boys in-studio on the day of the winner announcement,' I said. 'The full list of finalists is underneath the cake and there are plenty of boys there who might tickle your fancy. Once you've eaten your way through the cake, just let me know which finalists you'd like and I'll have them in the Green Room at 7.45 am on announcement day looking buff and ready to go.'

Piece of cake.

Emerging back onto Martin Place I bumped into the host of Six's *Newsnight* on my way to the car. 'Hey, Aaron,' I called. 'I just dropped off a ginormous chocolate cake with the *Wake Up!* production crew. If you're quick you might just grab a slice before they devour it. I know what a sweet tooth you have . . .'

'Thanks, gorgeous,' he replied, winking and flashing his best TV-presenter smile.

It couldn't hurt to have *Newsnight* and *Wake Up!* battle it out for exclusive coverage of my bachelor boys. A bit of intra-network competition never hurt anyone. Not to mention the rival networks that were also on my hit list. 'Oh, and the boys will be appearing at a media briefing at the Beresford tomorrow, babe. You should come along. If you're not too scared you won't measure up,' I added cheekily, knowing I'd just guaranteed myself a *Newsnight* crew at the event.

My phone vibrated inside my limited edition LV handbag (fluorescent graffiti style, of course). Whipping it out, I scrolled through my latest emails as I left the giant red Six behind me. Work email, work email, work email, email from Luke about lunch (yes, please!), work email, work email, work email. And an email from Ben Gorman. Faaark, here we go . . .

From: Ben Gorman
Title: Head of Sales, Converse
Time: 12.48 pm

Hi Jasmine,
Just checking we're all square after the other night at Ivy? Sorry if I pushed your buttons. Insert lame excuse about being drunk here. You're the best PR Converse has had in a long time and I'd hate to jeopardise that over some stupid argument. Can I buy you a drink next time I see you on Converse business? I seem to recall you lost your last one.

Cheers,
Ben

Yes, Ben. Yes you can, I thought cheerfully. Because if there was one thing I didn't plan on doing it was crying over spilt caprioska. Not when my account with Converse was at stake. Sure, my flirtation with Ben was definitely over. And all before it really began. But what would I have done with a guy who didn't work overtime anyway? That sure as hell wouldn't have boded well for the bedroom.

Reply: *Apology accepted. I agree nothing should get in the way of the Converse/Queen Bee dream team. And as long as you send me the bill for your recent drycleaning costs, then it's a yes to that drink. I seem to recall you caught my last one.*

I hit send as I arrived back at my car, where I whipped off my parking ticket and jumped into the driver's seat. Honestly, who wrote paper parking tickets these days? Sydney City Council was so old-school.

Racing past CCP Magazines on my way to Surry Hills, I wondered how the rest of the Bees were getting on with their deliveries. As if reading my thoughts, Coast's delightful PR, Amanda, chose that moment to call me and update me on the Bees' handiwork.

'Jasmine!' her voice shrilled out of my hands-free. 'I'm at a photo shoot and someone has just walked into reception carrying a cake with a naked Coast doll on top!'

Fuck me. 'Keep your shirt on, Amanda. Your mini model might not be wearing his, but he *is* dressed in a bedsheet. And some very snug-fitting fondant undies if I recall,' I said.

'Jasmine! I don't care what baked goods his boxers are made from. He looks naked!' she shrieked.

I didn't have time for this today. 'Amanda, see for yourself. Just cut the damn cake,' I interrupted and hung up. I'd deal with her tomorrow.

Heading down Bourke Street, I resisted the temptation to continue on as far as the legendary Bourke Street Bakery and instead started looking out for the Beresford. Past Le Pelican French restaurant, past Emmilou tapas bar, past two Bees desperately trying to reserve a car space without the aid of a car. What the faark? Swerving to the side of the road, I pulled up next to the girls, only narrowly missing one seriously pissed-off driver who was not convinced saving a car spot with your body was a legitimate road rule.

'What the?!?' I tried not to laugh as I lowered my window to talk.

But Holly and Lulu were having none of that. Instead they both made for the passenger seat of my car, piling in on top of each other in a space so tiny even Ikea would have trouble finding a use for it. God bless the Smart car. I should think about replacing the Aston Martin with one of these. I'd never have to suffer another passenger again.

'Thank God you're here,' Lulu said from underneath Holly. 'You wouldn't believe what a nightmare it is to find a park around here.'

This was true. Scoring a legal unlimited parking space in Surry Hills is like spotting authentic Louis Vuitton in the Western Suburbs of Sydney. Finding six legal unlimited parking spaces in a row out the front of the Beresford Hotel – my mission for the Bees – was like trying to buy authentic LV in the Western Suburbs. Best take your plastic elsewhere, sweetheart.

'I know,' I sympathised. Fact was, it was Mercedes-Benz and not me that had insisted on there being a neat row of Smart cars out the front of the venue when the press arrived for tomorrow's media call. But that was only because they thought of it first. Which got me thinking. 'Loves, where's your Smart car?' I asked as we sped along Bourke Street.

'We dumped it near the Beresford,' said Lulu. 'And then went looking for a legal park on foot.'

Christ. Today was going to cost me a Goyard-handbag-sized fortune in parking fines.

As we drew closer to the Beresford I could see the offending car double-parked out the front, hazards flashing like a beacon to parking police everywhere. I swear I'd taught these girls everything they knew. As if proving my point, a Smart car suddenly came out of nowhere, swerving in front of me and nearly causing me to rear-end it.

'Shit!' I slammed on the brakes.

Alice blew me a guilty kiss and sped off before waiting for my reaction. Hot on her heels, Emma skidded around the same corner and nearly took off what little bonnet my Smart car had. In the front seat, Holly and Lulu screamed as I hit the brakes for a second time and nearly sent them through the windscreen.

'This is like a precision driving team,' I muttered and motioned to Emma to pull over so I could slide up alongside her. 'What the fuck?' was all I could manage and Emma looked relieved there were two car doors and two bodies between us.

'Sorry! We can't find parking anywhere!' Em offered by way of explanation for those at home who weren't following.

Before she could get any further there was a screech of tyres from behind and Alice (who must have set a land-speed record getting around the block) pulled up on the other side of me. 'I've got a plan!' she shouted over her blaring radio as we sat three abreast in the middle of one of Surry Hill's busiest streets. We were going to have to borrow driving demerit points from Lara Bingle at this rate. 'So, I've just done a lap round the Beresford and there's a construction site full of hot tradies right out the front,' she reported. While it was not unusual for my ladies to be checking out tradies, Alice's vision was hardly Grace Coddingtonesque in its design so far. 'And tradies clock off at 3 pm, right?' she said.

I checked my watch: 2.45 pm. Alice might be onto something here.

'So what if we ask the tradies *extra* nicely if we can have their parking spaces when they finish work? If they move just two trucks, there'd be plenty of room for our Smart cars. And I'm sure they'd be happy to help a Diesel-wearing damsel in distress, right?' Alice said, running a seductive hand over her denim-clad thigh.

'Genius. I love it,' I said.

Alice beamed.

'Get your arse over there now,' I instructed her. 'I always knew it would come in handy one of these days. The rest of us? We need to be ready to take the tradies' spots at 3.01 pm. And don't get arrested between now and then . . .'

Several minutes and just as many laps of the block later, six very smug Smart-car drivers pulled into parking spots out the front of the Beresford. Even Lulu managed to bunnyhop her way into a park. Sort of.

'Attrition by seduction,' I said, shaking my head at Alice. 'You've got a bright future in PR.'

'Thanks, Queen Bee,' Alice said. 'Just as long as I don't have to be here in the morning when the tradies arrive to find our cars are still here.'

I raised one eyebrow suspiciously. 'You told them their parks would be free in the morning?'

She nodded proudly and for the second time that day I was only peeved I hadn't thought of it first.

14

Hot men? Check. Strong coffee? Check. A completed checklist in my hands? Check. Screw Julie Andrews' raindrops on kittens, these were a few of my favourite things and they were all right here in front of me at the tX photo shoot this morning.

As if by divine intervention, the morning had dawned clear skies and sunshine for the second coming of the Coco Man of the Year Awards press junket. Normally I wouldn't do a media call the day after a stunt like our cakes, but this time I thought I'd take the chance. If there's one thing any girl in Sydney will tell you: when you've got a hot guy in the palm of your hand, you seize the day. Twenty hot guys? Carpe fucking diem.

Before the media call, however, there was this pesky photo shoot to do for the front cover of this afternoon's edition of tX street press. Which is how, despite my sins, I found myself standing on the corner of Oxford Street, with the Intersection shopping precinct behind me, supervising twenty hot boys performing for the camera. Hallelujah.

However, it wasn't quite Eden in this patch of Paddington. I did have Amanda to contend with. As a proud supporter of the Coco Awards, Coast was being represented at this morning's shoot by one of their male underwear models. And Amanda. Who was dressed for work in towering Peep Toe heels, so high she could barely teeter around on her pale skinny legs. *God, somebody give that girl a spray tan*, I thought idly as I watched her totter by. I'd choose orange over pasty any day.

While my twenty bachelors gave their best Zoolander impressions for the photographer, Amanda eagerly awaited the arrival of her (never-nude) Coast model. And what an arrival it was.

'Jesus Christ! Is that a coffin?' asked Claire, the tX reporter, as a large wooden box was delivered.

'He's here!' shrieked Amanda, managing to tear herself from the bachelors just long enough to welcome Cody the Coast model to the shoot. 'How are you, darling?' she called at full volume, as if the bloke in the wooden box was deaf not dead.

Wandering over to meet Cody, I realised why. The poor guy was actually encased inside a wooden Coast gift box, complete with hard plastic frontage.

'Can you breathe in there?' I shouted.

He smiled back at me and waved.

'Are you okay to do photos from inside?' I asked.

Cody smiled again.

Amanda sighed. 'Wouldn't you love a guy like this?' she cooed.

One kept in a soundproof box? Bloody hell, wouldn't any woman?

Standing with the early morning sunshine warming my back, I sipped my mocha and watched proceedings closely (sans sunglasses, unfortunately, as they seemed to have vanished from my handbag). The photographer had finally ushered all twenty guys – from footballers to fashion models, surf livesavers to socialites – into one long line snaking down the median strip for the perfect group shot.

Only it wasn't.

'Stop!' I shouted over the roar of cars on either side of the traffic island. 'Their T-shirts have to come off.'

'Settle down, J,' said Max the photographer, clicking away happily with the Victoria Barracks as his backdrop. 'The x in tX isn't a ratings guide, sweetie. Let me get a couple of shots of the guys with their kit on first.'

I shook my head firmly. 'No, shirts off,' I repeated. 'That blond one on the left there isn't wearing a Coco-branded T. As Coco mag's PR, I'm afraid I'm exercising right of veto. All shirts off.'

The guys shrugged and obligingly pulled off their shirts, causing passing drivers to honk and wolf-whistle and Amanda to dislocate her neck.

'I oughta speak to my union about these conditions,' Max said, winking at me, before returning to snap his semi-naked subjects.

However, as the boys were topless, there was now nothing in this shot that branded it as Coco. And any PR worth their salt wouldn't leave it to the subeditor to make sure their client was credited.

'Amanda, any chance we could get Cody in the main frame?'
I asked innocently. Cody's box bore a great big fuck-off *Coco Man
of the Year Awards* rosette on it. 'Rather than have Cody in an
individual shot, why not get him in the main pic too? That way,
by having him in every shot, you reduce the risk of Cody not
making the cover.'

'Good idea,' Amanda agreed. 'Then I also reduce the risk of
my boss kicking my arse.'

I steadied myself on a nearby traffic light. Agreement from
Amanda? Who knew it was possible? And all it took was an appeal
to her unabashed self-interest.

'Fab. Now how the hell do we move him?' I asked, turning
to Coast's crew of on-site handlers who were pretending not to
hear me.

Twenty minutes and two hundred kilograms later, Cody was
safely ensconced on the median strip with our finalists. Wooden
coffin and all. Admittedly, he did look a little hot and bothered
but so would you if you were lugged across one of Sydney's major
road arteries in a box.

'Brilliant, boys!' Max coaxed, snapping away while Amanda did
likewise on her BlackBerry. This was her kind of Kodak moment.
'Just a few more shots.'

By now Cody was really starting to swelter. His face was an
unnatural shade of red and beads of perspiration were visible
even from where we stood on the footpath.

'You – second from the end – just relax and let your arms
hang at your sides,' Max instructed a burly AFL player whose

biceps were thicker than my waist. He obediently dropped his arms. Cody wiped his forehead on his T-shirt sleeve.

'I want to try a shot with the guys walking across the road towards the camera,' Max called over his shoulder, not bothering to pause from his clicking. Jesus. This wasn't the Lane Cove Tunnel we were standing next to. Did he really want twenty of Australia's most eligible men to step out onto Oxford Street during morning peak hour? No wonder there was a bloody man drought in this city. Cody swayed in his box.

'Okay, Jazz and Amanda, I'll need you both to stand at the top of Glenmore Road and act as a roadblock to cars coming this way along Oxford,' Max ordered, indicating the intersection to our right where traffic was zooming past. Was my life really worth the cover of tX?

I should never give myself ultimatums when it comes to work because I found myself keeping pace with Amanda's Peep Toe stilettos as we trudged to the corner. Meanwhile, Cody rested his forehead against the front of his box, leaving a sweaty imprint on the glass. Amanda and I waited till the traffic lights turned red then teetered out onto the road, where we stood – arms outstretched and eyes squinted shut – and hoped that when the lights turned green the oncoming traffic wouldn't budge.

Cody chose this moment, in a daze of dehydration, to cool off by the only means available to him inside his sauna: he started removing his clothes.

'That's it! I've got the shot!' Max called delightedly as twenty perfectly sculpted men crossed the road towards him and Cody performed a striptease. 'I've totally got what I need!'

Max might have had what he needed – artistically and more – but Amanda and I were still holding back traffic with our bare hands.

'Uh, does that mean you're done?' Amanda called urgently to Max over her shoulder, unable to see what was going on.

'Yeah, babe,' came the reply. 'You should probably get off the road now. Everyone else has.'

Charming. At that, Amanda and I retreated to the footpath as fast as her Peep Toes would allow us, the onslaught of traffic close behind.

'Wanna check?' Max asked, allowing me to scroll through the images on his camera. I made a mental note to send the link to Shelley once the images were up on our blog. Burt Bacharach had it all wrong. *That's* what friends are for.

'Oh wow, Max. These pics look *amaze!*' I said. 'I can't wait to see them on this arvo's front page,' I reinforced.

Max nodded. 'Sure thing, sweetie. Bar H&M confirming they're opening in Sydney, nothing's going to trump twenty topless bachelors and Cody in his jocks for page one.'

Just what I wanted to hear. I only hoped Amanda and her never-nude protocol didn't catch it too.

To the strains of Eva Simon's 'Take Over Control' on the car stereo, my driver eased his car to the kerb, delivering me safely out the front of the Beresford Hotel. Having left my Smart car here with all the others overnight, I was taking no chances with parking and had instead opted for Queen Bee's preferred valet to get me to this afternoon's media call.

'Thanks a million, Carl,' I said, sliding out of the front seat and leaving a generous tip.

'Anytime for you, Jazzy Lou,' he replied as I made for the Beresford's rooftop beer garden, the scene of our press conference.

Trekking up the stairs and out onto the cobblestone courtyard on the roof, I was glad to have opted for Miu Miu wedges. Thanks, Shelley. Heels would be a nightmare up here. Proving my point, Emma and Anya, who were already setting up, had both dumped their shoes and were working barefoot.

'Okay, we need to put the podium and *Coco* banner over here, bosh and bosh,' I said, heading over to where they were working. 'Then there's enough room for the finalists to line up behind Leila Graham after they've been announced.' Leila was the editor of *Coco* magazine. 'Perfect photo opp. And there's just enough space for thirty-odd journos to squeeze in front of the podium,' I continued, thinking aloud. 'That way the media call looks packed from where the TV crews are filming back here.' As I gave instructions, I walked backwards away from the announcement podium and threw down a bunch of Nurofen tablets.

'Also, I've popped a spare copy of the press release into each goodie bag in case there's any anorexic hacks present who haven't eaten their way through their Coast cake yet,' I said. 'And the mobile photo booth is on its way so all press can have their pic taken with their fave finalist.' *And then publish the images on their websites,* I added mentally.

'The girls from the *Chronicle* will love that,' Em said. 'Any excuse to get up close and personal with the boys from *Bondi Rescue* without having to feign drowning first.'

By the time my feet were starting to ache in my Miu Miu wedges, I was worried. Very, very worried. It was ten minutes until show-time and there was only a rumour of journalists in attendance.

I dragged Em into the stairwell. 'Something's wrong,' I hissed desperately, hoping Leila and the rest of the gaggle from *Coco* wouldn't hear me. 'I know journos don't wear watches but this is ridiculous. There's like five people up there. If some of the dailies don't turn up soon, I die. And not in a Rachel Zoe way.'

Em didn't even try to talk me down. 'I know, love,' she said. 'And any telly crews that were coming should have had their cameras set up by now.'

This was true.

'I'm going to call Luke and see what's going down,' I decided. 'A bigger story must have hit. There's no other reason for the daily newspapers and weekly mags to do a no-show. And let's not even start on TV or radio.' Never had I seen a media conference buried like this. And I wasn't about to take it lying down. Grabbing my BlackBerry I stormed back up to the beer garden so at least Leila would see me going down with a fight.

'So where the bloody hell are you?' I shouted at poor Luke when he answered his phone.

'Oh, Jazzy sweetie, I'm so sorry I'm not there for your do,' Luke apologised. 'My editor's got me staking out her pad in

Double Bay. But why are you calling me now? Shouldn't you be in overdrive bossing people around right this second?' Subtle. Even if it was normally true.

'Why the fuck has your editor got you staking out her own pad?' I asked, confused. 'And I would be bossing the press around, if there was any press here to boss.'

'No press?' Luke gasped. 'Are you for real?' And then, 'Oh shit. That's why. They're all here.'

At his editor's waterfront unit? What the fuck? There was the screech of car tyres followed by the sound of Luke's car engine being switched off.

'I can't even park within five hundred metres!' Luke sounded exasperated.

'What's up with your editor?' I demanded.

Now Luke was confused. 'Didn't you hear me, Jazz? All the paps in Sydney are here. It's not just her.'

This was baffling. Luke's editor was better known for her sharp-tongued celeb assassinations than her daytime soirées. Why the hell had she come over all Donna Hay today of all days?

Suddenly it dawned on Luke. 'OMG! You haven't heard, have you, hon?'

Finally. This I understood. 'No,' I said bluntly. 'I haven't.'

'I'm staking out *Belle Single's* flat, not my editor's. Word on the street is Belle Single has a new man. And not just any man. Her BFF's ex-fiancé! A tip-off went out that the happy couple have been holed up in her flat for days, à la Warnie and Liz, so everyone is down here trying to get the scoop.'

Fuck. 'I've gotta go, Luke.'

'Chin up, babe.'

Outrageous. One man dangles his dongle in front of Single and our twenty bachelors are blown out of the water. This stunt had to be the work of Diane Wilderstein. Why else would Belle come over all John and Yoko today of all days? It seemed a hell of a coincidence. Especially when you considered that Diane would be gagging to get some publicity coverage up and happening for Belle. Plus, anyone who was anyone in the Sydney press scene would have received our media alert about today's conference. Anyone like *Eve Pascal* editor and good friend of Wilderstein PR, Lillian Richard. It wouldn't have been hard for Diane to find out about our plans today. Seemed like it wasn't so tough for her to ruin them either. All she'd had to do was convince Belle Single to jump into bed with her best buddy's sloppy seconds. We didn't stand a chance.

But how would I tell the Bees? How would I explain that we'd been trumped by the Shire tramp? Not to mention what I would say to our clients. Swallowing hard, I walked over to where the editor of *Coco* was on her mobile and motioned for her attention.

Leila nodded and wrapped up her call. 'I heard,' she said, solving my problem of how to start. 'Farking Single.' And then, 'If she thinks I'm sending my entertainment writer over there to snap her dirty laundry she's dreaming.' I admired her chutzpah.

'I promise we'll turn this around, Leila,' I said. 'Leave it with me. We may not have got the coverage we wanted today but Queen Bee will get things back on track.'

Leila clearly wasn't convinced but was polite enough not to disagree out loud. 'I'll leave you to explain to the press that did turn up,' was all she said before leaving with her posse from the mag.

Turns out it only takes minutes to cancel a media call compared with the weeks involved in organising one. As we armed our bummed guests with as many goodie bags as they could carry, I promised to shoot them a media release explaining all later today. God only knew what I'd write in that. I slumped down onto a bench in the beer garden and Em plonked herself next to me and handed me a glass. I swear that girl has a bevvie for all occasions. 'A martini?' I asked half-heartedly, smelling the alcohol before I could taste it.

'Shaken not stirred. Just like you, love,' said Em. 'The bartender did offer me the special of the day but I figured a "Group Hug" wasn't really your style, with or without Zubrowka Vodka.'

'No, I'm feeling a little more "Harvey Wallbanger",' I conceded. 'Shit, Em. How did this happen?' I asked, watching our bachelors file downstairs to the bar in the stuff of an NRL publicist's worst nightmare. 'We had the pièce de résistance of Australian hunks here today and we still couldn't get the media to come. Was there more we could have done?'

Em stabbed at the olive in her drink.

'What's wrong with this fucking city today?' I went on. 'Honestly. This is Sydney. Sydney! This is the city where being attacked by a shark might be the end of your arm or your leg but it's just the beginning of your career as a male underwear model. The city where you might be jailed for conspiracy to murder but if you're blonde and hot and sporting a European accent you can move from Long Bay to Double Bay faster than you can say "parole". This is the city where your mates have modelling contracts, the models have designer clothing lines and the designers have the keys to the city. Sydney is the vain and narcissistic capital to rival all other vain and narcissistic capitals. We make London look like a UN ambassador and New York a Nobel Peace Prize winner. Since when did twenty semi-naked male models not rate in Sydney?'

Back at QB HQ, I was still reeling from this morning's floor-wiping from Belle Single. The Bees, however, were reeling from a surfeit of Lindt chocolates. A girl's gotta keep morale high somehow, right?

Staring despondently at the blank media release template document on my screen I groped for the words to explain this morning's debacle. *COCO MAN OF THE YEAR AWARDS PLAY JAKE WALL TO BELLE SINGLE'S JEN HAWKINS?* Not exactly the headline I'd had in mind when we launched the campaign. Distracted, I toyed with my takeaway matzo ball soup in its plastic bowl until Lulu interrupted me.

'I've got Amanda from Coast on the line for you, Jazz.'

Oh, someone drive me to the Gap, will you? I can take it from there, I swear.

'Thanks, put her through, Lulu,' I said.

'Jasmine, we've got to stop press on tX,' Amanda said breathlessly, not even bothering with the niceties.

'Pardon?' was the best I could manage.

'We've got to stop tX from going to print. Their photographer, Matt —'

'Max,' I interrupted.

'Max,' she repeated. 'He just sent me through the images from this morning's shoot and Cody is practically naked!'

Oh, that.

'So were you happy with the pics? Cody sure can fill a pair of Coast briefs.'

'Jasmine, we need to stop press now!' She was starting to sound hysterical.

'Look, Amanda,' I reasoned, 'as much as I feel for you – what with you being the only Coast representative at a shoot where the Coast protocol was so blatantly stripped away, so to speak – we can't hit pause at 2.45 pm on a newspaper that hits stands at 3 pm. Today's tX will already be stocked at train stations across the city, just waiting for the tX promo girls to strut their stuff.'

'I don't care!' Amanda screeched. 'Can't your girls go and stop them?'

I had a brief image of the Bees doing battle with tight-T-shirt-wearing promo girls at stations across the greater metropolitan area. Like *Sucker Punch* does CityRail.

'No, Amanda. They can't.'

'Shit. Well, it better not be on the front cover,' she said, which was quite possibly the first and last time I'd ever hear those words uttered by a publicist.

'Right. Let's hope we're not page one,' I agreed, marvelling at the parallel PR universe I'd stumbled into. Would Kyle Sandilands be capable of good press here? The mind boggled. 'I've gotta go, Amanda,' I signed off.

'Later,' came the response as Amanda hung up.

Seriously. That girl put me off my matzo balls.

As I toyed with my takeaway and replayed in my mind the conversation with Amanda, Em appeared at my office door, a glossy mag in hand.

'Am I going to like this?' I began, wincing in expectation as Emma proffered the latest copy of *Eve Pascal* magazine, its lustrous pages shining under the harsh overhead ceiling lights.

Em shook her head, cringing.

I braced myself and extended an arm. Em handed over the offending glossy.

Flipping the mag the right way up I found myself face to face with one very sultry, very pouty sloe-eyed Belle Single. Seducing the brave citizens of Sydney one newsstand at a time, I thought wryly.

'Belle bloody Single.'

Emma grimaced in support.

'Well, what a surprise to see her cosmetically enhanced face on the front cover of *Eve Pascal*. I suppose I'm meant to think it's a happy coincidence that Belle's smug mug features on the very issue that hits stands the day she's caught in a sordid tryst,' I fumed. 'It's like Lillian Richard knew Belle was going to be busted on publication date. Uncanny, isn't it?' I added sarcastically.

Em's eyes widened. 'Surely you don't think Diane set this up with Lillian just to fuck up our press conference today? Paranoid much, Jazz?'

I shook my head vigorously. 'You don't know what Diane's like, Em. The woman probably bites the heads off orphaned kittens before she sits down to breakfast each day. Squashing my press conference wouldn't even rate a diary note in her daily reign of terror, so hectic is her schedule of atrocities.'

Em stifled a giggle at my hyperbole. Easy for her. She'd never had to face Diane. It was like staring down Lucifer.

'Plus,' I slammed *Eve Pascal* and Belle Single's face down on my desk for emphasis, 'it's not like Lillian Richard hasn't been using my headshot as target practice lately. Ever since our run-in over the *Eve Pascal* Awards for fashion and beauty Lillian has been gunning for me.'

'And Diane was only too happy to supply the bullets,' Emma finished for me.

'Bullseye,' I agreed. 'Only, there's no straight shooting when Belle Single gets involved. Her best friend's ex-fiancé? That stuff is twisted!'

Emma laughed. 'You wouldn't need to look far to find the smoking gun, would you?' She changed tack. 'So what do you plan to do, Jazzy Lou? Retaliate? Or do you reckon this is a parting shot from Lillian? She won't take it further, surely?'

I sighed. 'No, she won't. The *Eve Pascal* lot need us as much as we need them, so I can only assume that Lillian has made her point and now is the time for a ceasefire. Besides, even if Diane hadn't arranged Belle's bed-in for today, there was no way Lillian would have covered our event anyway. *Eve Pascal* and *Coco* are direct competitors, after all. It just sucks that they took the rest of the competition with them. I still can't believe we held a press stop and no press stopped by.'

Em saw the warning signs and before I could begin ranting again she started backing away towards the door. 'Shame, Jazzy Lou, shame,' she consoled.

As Em beat a hasty retreat I picked up *Eve Pascal* from where it lay on my desk and idly gave Belle Single a monobrow and moustache. Then I stopped myself. Why was I bothering to deface Belle when she'd done a good enough job of losing face with the public herself? Bonking her BFF's beau? Really? As far as publicity strategies went, this one was shockingly ill-advised and I wondered what the hell Diane was thinking. If, indeed, she was the one who dreamed it up. More likely the press had already got wind of Belle's bedroom antics and Diane had been forced to salvage the situation as best she could. Yes, the more I thought about it, the more I was convinced Diane wasn't *solely* to blame for Belle's misbehaviour. That honour lay partly at Belle's feet. Or a little higher up her anatomy.

15

If my Jewish grandmother, Bubbe, worked in the Queen Bee offices, she'd say we were cursed. Of course, if my Jewish grandmother, Bubbe, worked in the Queen Bee offices, a curse would be the least of our problems. For a start, there'd be her advice about my love life ('Get one') and her incessant self-commentary in the third person: 'Bubbe doesn't understand why you haven't met a nice Jewish boy, Jazmine.'

Luckily for all of us at Queen Bee HQ, Bubbe hadn't moved in. Unluckily, a curse had.

It started with simple things. Missing samples, deliveries that were never delivered to us, lost stock. But then things stepped up a little. Entire clothing rails of product started vanishing and then reappearing for sale on eBay. Cash was evaporating from desk drawers. As were jewellery, mobile phones and any other electronic item of value. Then one day, when a client arrived for a meeting at the Queen Bee offices and left relieved of her purse, it was time to admit the ugly truth: our curse looked an awful lot like a kleptomaniac.

Of course, what our thieving friend hadn't banked on was the fact that I was at the office by seven most mornings and rarely left before ten or eleven at night. Consequently, I was a human CCTV system and nothing that happened in the Queen Bee building could escape my beady eyes for too long. So by the time we'd seen more stock walk out the door than at an Alex Perry sample sale, I was pretty sure I knew whose sticky fingers were to blame: Holly's.

Holly had brought a little WAG *je ne sais quoi* to Queen Bee. Sadly, it seemed she had also brought with her a knack for swiping anything not nailed down. Like cash from my wallet the day I had a date with Ben Gorman. Or my Oliver Peoples sunnies before the tX shoot. Not surprisingly, I hadn't phoned Diane Wilderstein for a character reference before I'd hastily offered Holly a job at our Queen Bee anniversary party. If I had, I might have learned that – for once – Diane was wholly justified in getting shot of this member of her staff. Holly was a chronic thief and Queen Bee was just the latest in her long line of suckers. No wonder she'd been evasive about the reason she'd been sacked from Wilderstein PR. Fired for boardroom burglary isn't exactly the first thing you flag to a would-be employer. But now, at Queen Bee, it was time to catch a thief and I was certainly up to the task. Because, to misquote the inimitable Karl Lagerfeld, fashion's biggest bloodsuckers are light-fingered publicists.

First, however, a little pre-sacking sustenance was in order. Plonking myself down at a coveted table in Kawa Cafe, Surry Hills, I scanned the boho-organic menu while I waited for Luke to arrive. Two skinny mochas later, he made his entrance.

'*Ma chérie!*' he air-kissed. 'Are we channelling our inner Donald Trump today?'

I smiled wryly. That was sweet. But not really true. Because anyone who'd spent more than five minutes in my company knew my Donald Trump was much more *outer* than inner.

'You're fired!' I replied, a little too enthusiastically. I really was going to have to tone that down when I fired Holly.

'So tell me, Jazzy Lou,' said Luke, signalling for a waitress, 'how do you know Holly's your girl?'

I rattled off a list of indiscretions. Given that this culminated with the sentence: 'And then she was photographed in the social pages wearing an Allison Palmer one-off design that had been customised especially for me and is now missing from our showroom,' there wasn't much doubt in my mind.

Luke looked mortified. And well he should. Allison Palmer was our favourite client. 'Ah. That's fairly incriminating,' he offered.

Yes. Yes, it was.

'Will you lay charges?'

'There's no need,' I replied. 'When word gets out, this WAG's career will be red-carded anyway.'

Back at the office after breakfast, I popped a bunch of Nurofen and rehearsed my 'pack up your desk' address. While I had no doubt I had the balls to do this, the words proved a little more elusive. 'Holly, it's come to my attention your clients' products are getting more coverage on eBay than they are in the press . . .' Or: 'Holly, when I say I want you to *adopt* your client's style, I don't mean in a Brangelina-take-it-home-and-keep-it-forever kind of way . . .' Even, 'Holly, most people don't come to work with a balaclava and hessian sack . . .'

It was as I sat ruminating on my speech that I was interrupted by a series of loud bangs.

Gunshots! Jesus Christ, was Holly holding up the joint? I sprinted out of my office. 'What the fuck? Did you hear that?' I demanded.

The Bees looked at me like I was the one wielding a weapon. More shots were fired.

'That!' I exclaimed again. 'You heard that, right?' This time the Bees nodded.

Sirens kicked off somewhere in the distance and we all rushed to the floor-length dormer windows keeping sentry over the sleepy Alexandria street outside. Nothing. Not even a casual car-jacking. This was curiouser and curiouser. While our showroom here at Queen Bee saw as much celebrity traffic as the Ivy on Robertson Boulevard, LA, the rest of downtown Alexandria wasn't known for its bustling activity. Criminal or otherwise. Unlike Darlinghurst, where Wilderstein PR was located, and where I'd bravely taken my life in my hands every day I fronted up for work. And that was just *inside* Diane's office.

At the thought of Diane I wondered idly whether the shots outside our window could possibly have come from her trigger-happy gun finger. After all, it wasn't as though Diane wouldn't kill me given the chance. And she did have a shoot first, ask questions later policy when it came to human resources. Most likely, considering our proximity to the inner city, it was simply a drug-related crime. Fashion crimes tend towards the sartorial rather than the homicidal, after all.

Holly chose that moment to saunter into the office. Fresh from a little armed hold-up of a client somewhere, no doubt.

'What the –' she began when she saw us all standing by the window, but I cut her off.

'Holly? I'll see you in my office just as soon as my phone conference is done this morning.' I fully intended to uphold her right to remain silent, even if she didn't.

An hour later, as commanded, she appeared at my office door. 'Take a seat, Holly,' I began, idly wondering if she might walk off with the thing. I popped a handful of Nurofen and willed myself not to come over all Diane and utter the immortal words: 'Pack up your desk.' Instead I started with the much more obtuse: 'Holly, we need to talk about your office behaviour.'

Holly looked confused. She wasn't going to help me out here. Either that or she genuinely had no idea what I was talking about. That, however, didn't explain the Allison Palmer frock she was rocking in the weekend papers.

'Okay, Holly, why don't we start by listing some of the things that have gone missing from the office lately? You had realised things were going missing from the office lately, hadn't you?'

Holly nodded, giving nothing away.

At this point Lulu phoned from reception. 'Uh, Jasmine, I think you'd better come down here.'

'I'm in the middle of an arresting conversation right now, Lu. Can it wait?'

'It's the cops.'

Shit. What the hell were the police doing in my reception area?

'I'm on my way down,' I said to Lulu. I thrust a piece of paper and a pen at Holly with the instruction: 'Write me a list of stolen goods.'

Clattering down the stairs in my Miu Miu pumps, I imagined all sorts of scenarios waiting for me at the bottom. Holly had stolen something from the new Dion Lee collection. Or the whole collection. Or kidnapped Dion himself.

I turned on a high-wattage smile for the policemen slouched against our reception desk. 'Officers!' I greeted them, my hand shooting out to shake theirs. 'I hope my girls have been looking after you. What can I do for you?'

The officers barely cracked a smile. 'We're here about an alleged drive-by shooting that took place in Alexandria this morning. Did you hear anything?'

I breathed a sigh of relief. 'Oh, that!' I laughed. 'Yes, we had a drive-by this morning. Yes sir, we sure did.' The officers, however, failed to see the hilarity in this morning's shooting. I quickly went on, 'Uh, I didn't see anything. But I did hear shots being fired at about, oh, 9 am.'

One officer scribbled this down in his notebook.

'Any idea what the deal was?' I asked, showing all the concern expected of a model citizen.

'Drug-related, I'd say,' one cop mumbled, confirming my initial suspicions. At least I didn't have to worry about a murderous Diane barging through the showroom door. Not today, anyway.

'Mind if we have a look around?' the cop asked, as more officers wandered up the front staircase. In their wake I could see the beginnings of a roadblock outside.

'Of course,' I said. 'Be my guest. I'm afraid I've got a meeting to get back to but if you need anything at all, please just ask one of the girls.' The officers nodded. 'And Lulu, why don't you get the officers some water? They must be thirsty after working so hard to keep us safe and sound.' I pointed to a fridge filled with Queen Bee water bottles. No point missing a PR opp, is there?

Trekking back upstairs in my teetering heels, I was determined to see out my conversation with Holly before any more emergency services arrived. 'So how are you getting on with that list?' I asked as I walked through the door. 'Can you see what I mean now about things going missing?'

Holly sat slumped in her chair, her arms folded defensively across her chest and the piece of paper I'd given her lying blank on my desk. Fine. It was time to bust out a little Donald Trump.

'Holly, I saw you in the social pages at the weekend wearing my customised Allison Palmer gown. The same gown that went missing from our showroom last week. Any idea how you came to be wearing that particular dress? No? How about the wallet that disappeared from the boardroom when the reps from Mavi were here last week? Or Alice's iPod? What about the entire Body Science collection that went missing but later appeared for sale on eBay? Ringing any bells, Holly?'

Holly pouted her perfect WAG pout. 'You can't prove anything,' she said sullenly, waving a match dangerously close to my fuse.

'Holly, don't speak to me that way,' I sighed. 'It's insulting and it's unprofessional.'

The pout was unmoved.

'Holly, I've given you so many opportunities since you joined Queen Bee and you've responded by stealing from me – and your colleagues. I've got more than enough evidence to know it was you. I only thought you might come in here and be honest with me about it so we could end your contract on better terms.' Who was I kidding? We were hardly going to be having sleepovers and braiding one another's hair after I fired her. But now I had Holly's attention.

'You're firing me?' she asked incredulously. Wow. This kid might live under the same roof as an Olympic medal but she was hardly in the queue for a Nobel Prize.

'Yes, Holly. I'm terminating your contract. Effective immediately. How could I not? You stole from my clients. It's hardly PR 101. You're lucky I'm not pressing criminal charges.'

Holly nearly fell off her chair. 'You wouldn't!'

'Well, no. I said I wouldn't. But I'm very disappointed.'

'But you won't call the police?' She was panicked now.

'No, I won't call the cops.' As the words left my mouth, there was a knock on my office door. 'Stay there,' I instructed Holly as I went for the door.

They're strange, those moments in life when the literal and figurative worlds merge. Where your day becomes a cartoon strip and the words in one speech bubble are simply scooped up and turned into reality in the next box along. 'I hope Superman gets here soon!' you say. And *kapow!*, there he is in the very next picture. This sensation is rather like viewing a Romance Was Born design collection. You want a fashion show inspired by the 1980s cult classic *The Neverending Story?* Why, *kapow!*, here's a dress channelling Falkor, the giant flying dog-thing. Send an iced Vo-Vo down the catwalk, you say? *Kapow!* There goes a walking biscuit now. Looking for a nanna-blanket-slash-dress for the new season? *Kapow!* Your wish is my command. It's like, just by forming the words with your mouth, you somehow will them into being.

Or so it seemed when I opened the door to my office. Because standing patiently outside, notebooks in hand, guns in holsters, were two of NSW Police's finest.

'The cops!' Holly shrieked. 'You called the cops!'

I didn't call the cops. Nor did I have any idea I was opening my office door to reveal said cops. Of course they were the two very kind sirs I'd met downstairs ten minutes ago. Only, rather than explain this to Holly I simply said, 'Constables. Nice to see you again. Please come in.'

Before I could order an iced Vo-Vo (non-wearable) and a nice cup of tea for the officers, Holly was on her feet. She threw herself urgently in my direction, swung and launched two punches to my face in quick succession. Oh. My. God. Holly *punched* me? She punched me! I slumped to the floor. The officers grabbed Holly and slammed her against the door to my en suite bathroom. The room spun and I lay on the floor gasping for breath. Did that really just happen? Was I just punched by an employee? Twice? I cringed as I thought of the headlines in tomorrow's

Sun newspaper: *PR KO'D BY WAG. FASHIONISTA SPOTTED EATING! KNUCKLE SANDWICH ON THE MENU. QUEEN BEE SACKING HAS STING IN TAIL.* The press could never get hold of this one. At least, not unless it came from me.

'You all right down there?' One of the constables offered me a hand and pulled me to my feet.

Blood trickled from a cut above my eye. I glared at the twenty-four-carat black diamond knuckleduster decorating Holly's left hand. Holly glared at me. The cops, having determined that Holly was unarmed, unhurt and unlikely to deck anyone else, began to show signs of a sense of humour for the first time all day. 'Jesus, this the way you girls normally do business here? Board meetings with a bit of biff? We see less action in Kings Cross on a bad night.' Just what I needed. Comedy cops.

My head continued to bleed as one cop took down our details and the other towered over Holly. But I didn't have time for this: I had work to do. I reached for the press release on my desk to blot my bleeding face. 'It's fine,' I protested to the cops. 'I won't be pressing assault charges.' They looked at me dubiously. 'Really,' I insisted. Then I raised my bleeding head higher and uttered the words I should have said to Holly weeks ago: 'Just pack up your desk, Holly.'

I'd make sure she got her just deserts.

Cruising home in my Aston Martin that night I texted Shelley: *Need vodka, painkillers, bandage. On my way over, J x.* My head was still pounding after this morning's boxing lesson from Holly, but other than a few bruises, it looked like I'd survived unscathed. Nothing a little MAC makeup couldn't gloss over.

Which was more than I could say for Holly's career. Whoever said revenge was a dish best served cold hadn't tasted the piping-hot delicacies I'd whipped up this afternoon. Feeling hungry, fashionistas? Well then, why not try these tasty treats?

For entree, take one fresh BlackBerry, scroll through your contacts list vigorously, select the ripest, most influential members of the PR industry, then phone and offer a step-by-step description of Holly's manic kleptomania. Serve immediately. For main course, preheat Hotmail to around 180 degrees Celsius. Wash, chop and prepare one scathing email, complete with photo attachment of Holly (for identification purposes and just for spice), then roll out to every PR office and recruitment agency in the greater Sydney region. But save room for dessert! This deliciously decadent dish is worth ditching the diet over. Blend one list of stolen items with two quotes from aggrieved staff members, add a dollop of photographs (including a glamour shot of Holly and her famous fiancé), and garnish with a pic of the police leaving Queen Bee PR (as taken on your personal phone). Then spoonfeed to your favourite social columnist. Bon appétit!

But all this thought of food must have upset my delicate constitution.

Because the next thing I knew I was doubled over the steering wheel with searing stomach pain. Oh, gods of vengeance, is this you? Was my payoff for seeking payback against Holly a hernia? Could you catch karma cancer of the intestine? I clutched at my abdomen and gasped involuntarily. The pain was unbearable.

Slamming on the brakes and slapping on my hazards, I swung my door open and attempted to stumble from the car. Horns blared behind me and brakes screeched as motorists struggled to pull up in time. But I was too busy slumping over the bonnet of my sports car to notice. All I was aware of was the intense pain when I banged my already bruised and swollen face against the finely polished paintwork. This really wasn't my day. It was going to take a hell of a lot of Nurofen to dull this pain. Someone appeared beside me and made soothing noises along the lines of 'don't worry' and 'ambulance on its way'. I was hoping for 'stiff drink' and 'heavy-duty painkillers' but beggars can't be choosers. Then I blacked out.

Coming to in the back of an ambulance, I stared into the face of a squeaky-clean female ambulance officer, all swishy blonde hair and clear blue eyes and looking like she'd stepped out of a Lorna Jane sportswear brochure. I expected wheatgrass juice and goji berries to ooze out of her unclogged pores at any moment.

She in turn stared back at my blackened eye. 'Rough day?' she asked as she fed an intravenous drip of something I guessed wasn't alcohol into my arm.

'Had better,' I slurred. The jolting movement of the ambulance was doing nothing to stop my head spinning.

'You're lucky we got to you when we did,' Lorna Jane went on. 'I reckon you've got yourself a stomach ulcer there.'

I stared at her incredulously. 'A stomach ulcer?'

'Looks a lot like it,' Lorna Jane said perkily, her shiny blonde ponytail bouncing in time with the bumping of the ambulance.

'Ugh,' I groaned in reply.

'Have you suffered any nausea or vomiting lately?' the ambo asked. 'Or noticed any loss of appetite? Any weight loss?'

Was Lorna Jane kidding? I worked in *fashion*. If I wasn't seeing weight loss then I wasn't looking in the right places. As for loss of appetite – sheesh, I hadn't acknowledged hunger pains since the late 1990s. I wouldn't recognise my appetite now if it bit me on the arse.

'Uh, yeah that sounds vaguely familiar,' I said by way of reply. Lorna Jane wrote this down diligently.

I sat as still as I could to try to minimise the pain and to let the idea of a stomach ulcer settle. *How the fuck did this happen?* I wondered.

'Any idea how this might have happened?' Lorna Jane asked me, as if reading my thoughts.

I bit back several sarcastic responses. This woman was a medical professional and I was in charge of nothing more animate than a YouTube clip of BMW Australian Fashion Week and yet she was asking *me*? My head slumped to my chest.

'Okay,' she continued. 'Let's see if you can help me out here. Do you drink?' I nodded. 'Smoke? Take hard drugs? Ever self-medicate?'

At this I raised my head. 'Yes. I self-medicate.' I nodded again. 'Although never more than six Nurofen in any one sitting.'

The ambo dropped her clipboard.

'I'm in PR,' I added by way of explanation.

When the ambo finally got her jaw to work her words were not exactly welcome. 'You're in PR, huh? Well, not for a while you're not. A stomach ulcer is really serious. If it's burst you might need immediate surgery, and even if it hasn't, you certainly won't be back on your feet again for weeks.'

Weeks? I nearly fell off my stretcher. You've got to be kidding me, Lorna Jane. I couldn't take weeks off work! Hell, I couldn't take hours off work. I thought about the new Levi's account I was pitching for tomorrow morning and the Schwarzkopf Most Beautiful Hair event I was organising for tomorrow night. Then there was Fashion Weekend Sydney the following night and the Coco Man of the Year Awards looming fast after that. Of course, that wasn't to mention BMW Australian Fashion Week. I didn't have time for this. There was nothing in my schedule about a stomach ulcer and I wasn't having a bar of it.

'Immediate surgery, you say? So, what time will I be done?' As I reached for my BlackBerry, my IV drip wrenched out of my vein. Lorna Jane went into apoplexy so I offered her my drip.

'I don't think you understand! The surgery might be immediate but the recovery isn't. You won't be discharged from hospital this fortnight!'

Sure, Lorna, whatever you say, I thought as I dialled the number for my one next-of-kin emergency phone call. 'Em? It's Jaz . . . An ambulance . . . No, I'm fine. Just collecting emergency services experiences today . . . No, not for a campaign. Look, can you do me a favour? Can you postpone my meeting with Levi's tomorrow morning? No, afternoon is fine. Say, 2 pm . . .'

I shoved the IV line back in my arm, adjusted the bandage on my head and beamed a winning smile in the direction of Lorna's disapproving glare.

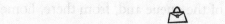

They came thick and they came fast. The sick, the wounded and the near-terminally drunk. They all staggered through the doors of the Prince of Wales Hospital that night until I was sure the sanitised, glaringly white Emergency Department was going to buckle under the weight of the wretched and collapse in a heap of broken limbs and ailing organs and crutches and sick bags and drug-fucked teenage girls from the Eastern Suburbs.

A triage nurse looked me up and down. I groaned quietly in agony. 'Jasmine Lewis?' she asked. I nodded. 'Suspected stomach ulcer, potentially burst,' she said aloud to no one in particular as she scrawled the diagnosis on a medical form.

'I'm sure it's not that serious,' I assured her, ignoring the stabbing pains in my abdomen. The nurse, in turn, ignored me. Apparently she didn't care for my esteemed medical opinion. Not when she had at least half a dozen screaming, vomiting or swearing patients lined up behind me, all of whom had appeared in the short time since the ambulance had dropped me off. I had no idea ER was so popular. At least not the version without George Clooney. I clutched my stomach and scanned the room. There sure as hell were a lot of people here. I wished I'd brought some branded Queen Bee bottles of water with me. Nothing like a captive customer base, after all.

'How bad is the pain, Jasmine?' the nurse asked, her harried voice free of any signs of compassion.

'It's a ten on the Richter scale, nurse,' I said, already planning my fast-track to the head of the queue and, from there, home and back to the comfort of my laptop.

'Ten?' the nurse confirmed, not looking up from her form.

'Ten.'

'Right, I've noted that down. Take a seat and a doctor will see you as soon as possible,' she instructed.

Take a seat? I pouted. Then lurched off to a row of nearby plastic chairs to wait. And wait. And wait.

Several hours later I was still slumped in my seat and showing no signs of going anywhere fast. If my stomach ulcer hadn't been burst when I'd arrived, it sure as hell would be soon, I thought grimly. Frustrated and near delirious with pain, I scrolled through my BlackBerry. Surely there was someone I could call to sort this out? I didn't have time to wait in a queue any more than I had time to have a stomach ulcer. I should be hitting the office in just a few hours. The contacts list in my phone didn't offer much by way of medical leg-up, however. Party planners, cake decorators, designers, couturiers, muses, fashion editors, beauty bloggers, the who's who of the Sydney social scene. But not a surgeon to be seen. Someone in the row behind me vomited violently onto the floor. Oh, this really was beyond.

Just as I was debating whether to take the spotty (and probably highly infectious) child beside me hostage and hold up the storeroom and medicate myself, a familiar voice called out from across the room. 'Jazzy Lou?'

My head snapped up. 'Samantha Priest?'

For the second time that evening, a blonde ponytail bobbed dizzyingly in front of me. Only this one was decidedly *less* squeaky clean than the one that greeted me in the ambulance. As was the person attached to it.

'What in the bloody hell are you doing here, babe?' she screeched affectionately, scuffing towards me across the lino, sick and dying people turning pale in her wake.

'Er, I think I may have a stomach ulcer,' I tried to say discreetly. The guy next to me shifted away in his chair as though he was sitting next to a leper. I looked pointedly at the spotty child in his lap.

'Shit, eh?' called Samantha. 'That's rooted.'

Quite, I thought, idly wondering whether Samantha was here to have her excessive Australian vernacular gene removed. She seemed to have been born with more than her fair share.

'And you?' It seemed only polite to return the question. And much as the Emergency Department at POW Hospital was not where I would have chosen for our rendezvous, I *was* glad to see her.

'Had me stomach pumped. *Again!*' She laughed at the folly of her situation. 'One too many bourbon and cokes at Ravesi's. LOL!' she added. The remnants of charcoal skirting round her mouth suggested some other form of decontamination but I let it slide. Instead, I nodded like it happened to me all the time.

And then I did the maths on that. 'Let me get this straight: you've been to Ravesi's, had time to get wasted, been through ER and had your stomach pumped. *Already?*' I asked incredulously. 'What time did you start drinking? Breakfast?'

Samantha laughed and tugged at her cotton shift dress. Even in the middle of the night in ED, dressed only in beach wear, she still managed to look like a model. 'Nah, babe. I didn't get to Bondi till late. But I've got contacts here so they don't make me hang around.' She inclined her blonde head towards the queue of patients now snaked out the doors of Emergency.

I sat up straighter in my plastic chair, sending shooting pains through my abdomen. 'Contacts?' I yelped.

'Yeah, I slept with one of the registrars here. Cute guy but way too brainy for me. Like being stuck in an episode of *Grey's Anatomy*.'

I pulled myself out of my seat and clutched at Samantha's arm. 'Take me to him!'

'Sure thing, babe. But I never thought you'd be one for sloppy seconds.'

'The good news is the PUD in your duodenum is not perforated as suspected.'

I squinted in concentration. Clearly the drugs had inhibited my ability to understand English because that last sentence didn't make a whole heap of sense when received by my throbbing head.

'Of course, the bad news is obviously that the diagnosis is a peptic ulcer, probably caused by NSAIDS or anti-inflammatory medications.'

Nope, no good. Not a language I could understand. I stared in incomprehension at the registrar, who'd come to visit me the next day. No wonder Samantha Priest had had trouble with this guy. God knows what their pillow talk involved.

I held my hand up to indicate he should stop talking. 'Again?' I requested.

'You've got a stomach ulcer but the stomach ulcer hasn't burst,' he said flatly. 'That was the upshot of the gastroscopy and the barium meal we gave you this morning.'

Oh, the barium *meal*. That I understood. How could I forget the revolting chalky goo I'd so recently had to force down. It was the first square meal I'd eaten in weeks.

'So,' the reg went on, 'I'm recommending a short-term course of antibiotics and a long-term course of proton-pump inhibitors. Plus close observation in hospital for at least the next few days.'

I gasped.

'And lay off the Nurofen tabs,' he added categorically.

No Nurofen? Incarcerated for at least the next few days? Fuck, it was like a kibbutz in here. And this reg was the head zealot. What had Samantha Priest ever seen in him? Other than his willingness to support queue jumpers in ED, that was. A handy perk if you got wasted as often as Samantha did, I guessed.

I rolled over haughtily in bed, grabbing uselessly at my hospital gown in a vain attempt to achieve some semblance of dignity.

'Nice arse, babe!'

WTF! I nearly toppled off the narrow hospital bed in shock as I scrambled to cover my cavorting cheeks. Weren't there laws against a lack of doctor/patient decorum?

'So are you hot to trot now or what?' Samantha Priest bounded into the room, her appraisal of my anatomy arriving before she did.

'No, she's not,' interjected Doctor Fun.

I couldn't tell who was annoying me more, him or her.

'And she won't be for several days,' he added.

I let out a sigh of frustration.

'Oh, too bad, huh?' Samantha consoled, then in the next breath: 'So, are you ready to split, sweet cheeks?'

I grabbed at my hospital gown again.

Samantha laughed. 'Not you, Jazzy Lou!' and she slipped a hand under the registrar's scrubs before manhandling him out the door.

Over the next few days I made life hell for the poor nurses assigned to care for me, refusing to lie down and take my prescribed medicine quietly.

Instead, I moved the Queen Bee offices into Ward E of Prince of Wales Private Hospital.

'No, no, that's not enough,' I blasted down the phone. 'We need at least double that amount of imported limes and we need them before Friday.'

A pause while the person on the other end responded was punctuated by the beeping of some complex-looking machine to my right.

'No, I won't take limes from the Riverina! This is a Hawaiian-themed event and I want my limes to come from the North Pacific!' Honestly.

I punched the red phone symbol on my BlackBerry, nearly reefing my IV line out at the same time. The machine beside me beeped angrily. Maybe it was a heart-rate monitor after all . . .

'Imbeciles!' I huffed to Em, who sat perched on the end of my hospital bed, iPad in hand. Em busied herself reading publicity schedules.

We had less than two weeks to go now until the VIP (and Hawaiian-themed) *Coco* Man of the Year Awards event. And not much longer until Allison Palmer's show at BMW Australian Fashion Week. I needed to haggle over limes like I needed a proverbial hole in the head. Or a literal one in the stomach. Anya, Alice and Lulu wandered into the room, fresh from an excursion to the hospital canteen.

'It was *dire*,' announced Alice, flopping onto the empty bed beside me. My BlackBerry rang again loudly just as Em's mobile buzzed and yet another delivery of flowers arrived at the door.

'Lulu, can you get those?' I indicated the enormous bunch of gerberas blocking the doorway, a pair of delivery-man legs sticking out below. Lulu nodded and turned to the door. 'And remember,' I directed while picking up my ringing BlackBerry, 'cut the stems pre putting them in water. And make sure you add some sugar to the water. And one colour per vase — *never mix them*, okay? Hello, Jasmine Lewis speaking . . .'

Lulu struggled under the weight of my OCD directions as she grappled with the flowers.

A nurse squeezed past her and entered the room, muttering, 'I thought this was POW not QB HQ,' to no one in particular, which was lucky because no one in particular was listening.

'Leila, hi!' I enthused down the phone. It was Leila Graham, editor of *Coco*, wanting to talk turkey about our kitten of a Man of the Year Award winner: Kurt Simmons. Kurt was an e-entrepreneur whose main claim to fame was dreaming up an online adoption process for rescued pooches. And while the women of Australia may have chosen him as their fave eligible bachelor, Kurt certainly wasn't going to win us any friends in the press. I mean, how the hell was any self-respecting journo going to fill a feature interview with Kurt Simmons? Ask him about his Boy Scout badges? Reveal his heady anecdotes of helping little old ladies across the road? Tap his boringly reliable phone conversations to his mum each Sunday night? Hardly the stuff of news headlines.

Em pulled up Kurt's publicity strategy on the tablet in front of her and swung it around for me to read while I spoke to Leila. It was a short document.

'Okay, what we need is a new, improved bad-boy angle on Kurt,' I began. 'The media have done the "protector of parentless poodles" story to death. We need to give them something hot, something risqué, something they never knew about Kurt before. The Kurt I'm thinking of is a little less Von Trapp and a little more Cobain.'

'Fab, babe, I love it,' interjected Leila. 'But how do you plan to do that?'

I paused. 'Sit Kurt next to one very glamorous but very unlucky-in-love social-pages junkie at the event and sparks – then headlines – are sure to fly.'

'Genius,' Leila purred. 'Absolute genius, Jazz. Do you have someone in mind? I can't wait to see that in action.'

Neither could I. If only I could get out of this bloody hospital in time to witness it.

The nurse, who was still fussing around my room, chose this point in our conversation to inform me, in no uncertain terms, that I should get off the phone. She did this by removing said phone from my ear and hanging up on Leila for me.

'Hey –' I started indignantly, but the nurse wasn't having a bar of it.

'Jasmine Lewis,' she instructed, 'you need to make a few lifestyle modifications if you want to avoid ending up in Emergency again. Lifestyle modifications like stressing less and sleeping more and,' she reefed open the top drawer of my bedside table and swiped my latest box of Nurofen Plus, 'kicking your ibuprofen habit fast.' I sulked as she made her way around the room, throwing curtains open and throwing Bees out into the corridor. 'You can't expect to recover if you don't give your body time to rest!'

I paused to consider my options. The way I saw it I had a pretty clear choice: a) Put my Miu Miu-shod feet up. Perhaps book myself into some exey, unsexy, organic, hippie spa retreat and drink coconut water till I looked like an extra on *Cast Away*; or b) Put my Miu Miu-shod foot down, continue to work my arse off and maybe – just maybe – I'd pull off the best damned Coco Man of the Year Awards and BMW Fashion Week show this town had ever seen and assure Queen Bee's survival in the process.

Of course, there was a third, less appealing option involving a burst stomach ulcer, some emergency surgery and a slow and painful recovery. But best not to dwell on that here.

Fact was, stomach ulcer or no stomach ulcer, I wasn't about to bite the dust for anybody.

Daphne Guinness, celebrated style icon and kooky aunt of the fashion fraternity, once said, 'I don't approach fashion; fashion approaches me!' I felt much the same way about disaster. We were beginning to look tighter than Sass and Bide, disaster and I. Always clutching one another's arms and finishing one another's sentences whenever we appeared in public. So now, having been beaten up by an employee and knocked down by a stomach ulcer, I was pretty much ready for disaster and me to part ways.

I staggered up the front steps of Queen Bee that afternoon, straight out of a cab from the hospital, and struggled through the heavy glass door. The chandelier in reception reflected my own bedraggled image, my not-quite-faded black eye winking back at me a thousand depressing times. But I'd survived several nights in hospital and just as many days away from the office (the two things

211

on a par in my mind), and now, contrary to doctor's orders, I'd signed myself out of hospital and was back at the Queen Beehive.

Which was where I found myself face to face with a new-season Rebecca Thompson creation hanging blithely in a courier bag at reception, ready to be whisked away to a fashion editor. *Wrinkled.*

'Why has this garment not been steamed?' I bellowed, stalking into the showroom, the offending dress dragging behind me. Laughter died where it fell and it was mourned by stunned silence. 'What?' I demanded. 'You didn't seriously think I was going to stay in hospital all week? Have you seen what a hospital gown does for your figure?'

I switched on both my computers. 'Oh, and Alice?' I added, not looking up from my screens. 'Those look-books need to stay up the back of the showroom. You know how I like things to match.' Honestly, a few days away from the place and everything turned to shit.

Bang on cue, Amanda chose this moment to phone me from Coast Underwear. 'Jasmine!' she gushed. 'How *are* you? It's been far too long.'

Had it? I couldn't tell you. I hadn't exactly been counting down the days in my Bottega Veneta diary until we spoke again.

While she jabbered away I tidied the Queen Bee garment bags that hung on a giant roll near my desk, like supermarket bags on steroids. Not that I did my own grocery shopping, but I'd seen how it worked in an episode of *Australia's Next Top Model* when the models took an excursion to Coles.

'Jasmine, I need to talk to you about the seating arrangements for next week's *Coco Man of the Year Awards*,' Amanda said.

'I've been thinking −' I braced myself. 'Why don't we abandon the current seating plan and have everyone sit at one long table together? Like a Heston Blumenthal banquet but bigger! Wouldn't that be fun?'

My head throbbed and my stomach ached. I should have got some morphine to take away in a hospital doggy bag. That would have been fun. Pumping the stuff through my veins till I could no longer hear the words coming from Amanda's mouth would have been fun. But redoing the seating arrangements for four hundred special guests, celebrities and media personalities a few days before an event? That would not be fun. That was not even close to fun and I told Amanda so.

'Sorry, A, no can do. I'd rather hang myself with my new Hermès belt than make changes now. The current arrangements are final.'

Or so I thought.

It's funny, that word final. Look up the *Macquarie Concise* and there, listed with a neat little *adj.* next to it, is this: 1. *relating to or coming at the end; last in place order or time.* Not: *Last in place order or time until someone else messes with it.* Or: *Last in place order or time until someone comes in and fucks it up by switching all the place cards thereby screwing the seating arrangements.* My guess was that certain someone had straggly blonde hair extensions and a name starting with 'A' and ending with 'manda'. Because when I made my entrance into the Grand Ballroom at the Ivy several days later − bespangled from blonde roots to ankle boots in silver, sparkly, sequinned

Ellery and ready to witness the crowning of Coco's Man of the Year — what I thought was the final seating plan proved not to be. Around me, the rest of the room whirled on. Beautiful girls with deep golden tans and long, long synthetic blonde hair stalked past pretending they couldn't tell you were watching. Snappers hustled through the crowd and waitresses tottered past carrying trays of cocktails decorated with kitsch umbrellas. And there, among the pineapples and palm trees of this evening's Hawaiian theme, the seating arrangements had been changed. Gah! My plan to score Kurt Simmons some headlines — and a date — would be sunk if I didn't rearrange the rearranged place cards. And fast. Stalking over to where our winner was supposed to be sat, I began hunting around for his name tag when I stumbled upon my own. Gah again!

Now, rather than sitting surreptitiously by the door so I could spend all night slipping out and monitoring events backstage, I was slap-bang in the middle of the room. Much worse, though, were my dining companions. You know when unimaginative journalists ask the question: 'Who, dead or alive, would you most like to invite to a dinner party?' That night it was as though someone had found my list, scrolled straight to the very bottom and then set the table accordingly. I swear I'd rather have plated up for Galliano than broken bread with those on my table that night. There was not a single person in my immediate vicinity that I wouldn't have preferred dead than alive.

For starters, to my right was sat the PR ambassador for Coast Underwear Australia, one Amanda Worthington. This arrangement promised an evening of banal conversation, possibly peppered with a PR disaster or two, and all caused solely by Amanda's ineptitude. And to my left? Why, there was that other ambassador of men's underpants (by reputation at least) – Belle Single.

'Belle Single!' I hissed down the phone to Luke, who was on the far side of the room interviewing celebs for the social pages. '*Belle Single!*' I repeated for effect. 'What the hell is Belle Single doing here?' Had Amanda forgotten Ms Single singlehandedly sabotaged our press conference for this very event by staging a love-in with her best friend's ex-fiancé?

Luke laughed. 'Babe, Belle Single is like the mascot for man-hunters. You can't host a male meat market in metropolitan Sydney and not expect Single to show. Trust me, she can sniff it out!'

I sighed and took a swig of my mai tai cocktail.

'Anyway, who else is sitting with you?'

I turned to inspect the remaining place cards on the table. 'Uh, Michael Lloyd, whoever that is. And – '

Suddenly, a lone figure appeared before me. A lone figure with a new-season Birkin. A lone figure that struck fear into the very core of my heart and made me forget, temporarily, about my plan for Kurt.

'Diane!' I gasped, my phone still glued to my ear.

'Diane?!' Luke shrieked down the line.

'Jasmine,' she said flatly, her hands too occupied with her enormous Birkin for anything as civil as a handshake.

'What are *you* doing here?' I blurted, dropping my BlackBerry (and poor Luke) to the floor. 'And at *my* table?' I added, narrowing my eyes. Suddenly I doubted it was Amanda who had switched the table arrangements.

Oh, why did Diane keep doing this to me? I wondered, thinking ruefully back to her unwelcome appearance at Queen Bee's first-anniversary party. Of all the fucking gin joints . . . Why on earth was Diane seated at my table? Alongside Amanda Worthington and Belle Single! It was like the ghosts of Christmas past in here. Happy fucking Chanukah, I thought grimly.

Diane sniffed and pushed her Hermès black leather bracelet back up her bony arm. I adjusted my Givenchy leopard-print cuff in reply. Our rearmament complete, we headed into battle.

'What am I doing here? Oh, Jasmine, there are publicists other than you with clients here tonight. Or potential clients, anyway,' she said cryptically. 'In fact, there are still entire PR firms eking out a living in this city alongside Queen Bee PR,' she sneered.

I nearly choked on my mai tai in delight. Eking out a living? Diane was eking out a living? Don't tell me Wilderstein PR was feeling the sting of Queen Bee's blossoming PR presence? Don't tell me she was hurting because of little ole me? Each and every morning that I'd hauled my arse out of bed and into the office since QB PR began suddenly shone golden in my memory. It was like those TV ads where they wipe over the kitchen in one easy motion and the whole thing glistens and sparkles. If Diane was hurting, then my every effort had been worth it. I didn't even try to suppress my smile.

'Of course there are,' I gloated unashamedly. 'It's just we're getting so busy at Queen Bee these days that we forget all about the competition. Now, if you'll excuse me, I've got to check on a few things backstage. You understand.'

Diane scowled and I hotfooted it before she had the chance to wrap her Hermès leather bracelet neatly around my neck.

Backstage, however, things had gone awry.

The five hundred gift bags we'd couriered over early that day had been unceremoniously dumped on the floor of the green room, like the Mount Fuji of freebies. Beside them sat an unopened box containing one thousand individually wrapped gourmet macaroons. All of which were supposed to be inside the offending gift bags. Gah!

It was time to do what I do best.

'Um, can someone tell me what is going on here?' I shouted. 'Someone? Anyone? You!' I screeched at a hapless cable runner who had made the mistake of being in my firing line. 'I want you, you and you to tidy this up now,' I continued, pointing at two other randoms who were hanging out backstage. 'And Lulu and Alice,' I said, spying some Bees nearby, 'help me sort out these biscuits. Now!' Kurt's place card would have to wait a bit longer.

I took a deep breath, kicked off my shoes and bent down and got to work. I was in the middle of running an Isabel Marant-clad knuckle down the seam of the macaroon box to slice it open when I heard the swish of sequins behind me.

'Doll!' came a plummy voice from inside the sequins. A voice I'd recognise anywhere.

'Pamela Stone! My favourite gossip queen! What brings you backstage?' I kicked a gift bag out of the way with my foot.

'Oh, I live for backstage. Everybody's a nobody until you get backstage,' she said, laughing.

I stood, barefoot, and brushed cookie crumbs from my gown.

Pamela had enough class to pretend not to notice. 'Now, doll, I've heard talk that you had some kind of epiphany while holed up in hospital. You know, detoxing and soul-searching and generally turning all zen and Miranda Kerr on us. So is it true Queen Bee PR is up for sale now?'

My mouth fell open.

'And that you'll settle for ten million because you're downsizing and sea-changing to somewhere more coastal? Like Tamarama? What's the story there, doll?'

Now I had to laugh. Even by Pamela's standards this was impressive. The tabloid talent was always first with the goss but this rumour was so fresh even I didn't know I was selling. In fact, I wasn't sure what surprised me most – the idea that I was selling Queen Bee or the fact that the social pages knew about it before I did. Not to mention the thought of ten million dollars.

'Ah, sorry to disappoint you, Pamela, but nothing could be further from the truth. Queen Bee is not on the market. And I'm not in the market for a life overhaul.'

That last part was probably not strictly true, but Pamela, bless her, looked relieved anyway. 'You're sure, dear?'

I nodded emphatically.

'And what about the ten million? Is that bit true?'

I was tempted to nod again. While there was no way in hell my business was worth anywhere near ten big ones, there was also no way Diane Wilderstein would ever miss one of Pamela's columns. And I'd love to give Diane something to stew on over breakfast.

'I'm afraid I can't comment,' I replied sweetly. 'It's so crass to talk about your millions once you pass double figures, don't you think?' Oops.

Leaving Pamela to spread that salacious story, I was on my way back into the Ivy Ballroom when Shelley texted: *Dah-ling, in the bath with a vino and the Man of the Year edition of Coco magazine. Now, here's a fun reconnaissance mission. If I select my fave hot bod, will you find him in the flesh for me tonight? Mwah.*

LOL. This was too good. Was Shelley seriously going to lie in the bath and text me her wish list from the finalists so I could then seek him out for her at tonight's event? This was like *Where's Wally* does RSVP. And what would I do when I found him? Tell the lucky guy my friend fancied him? And that she was already at home naked, in case he was interested?

Sure, babe. Just send me a pic, I replied, although I could already imagine her selection.

Turned out I didn't need to wait long. Within seconds Shell had sent me through an image. Of herself. Lounging luxuriously in her bathtub and artfully clad in a bikini of bubbles.

Not of you! I shot back. *A pic of the guy you want me to find! What the hell am I supposed to do with pornographic images of my best friend?* I hit delete fast.

Back in the ballroom I accosted a waitress and grabbed myself a glass of champagne. And not just to recover from the picture I'd just seen. If I had to go back to my table – and down a few rungs in Dante's Inferno – I was damned if I wasn't doing it well lubricated. I was about to resume my quest for Kurt's place card when across the room I spied something to make me choke on my Chandon. There, in the corner, was Diane talking earnestly to Allison Palmer. My designer, Allison Palmer. My soon-to-be-rising-star-of-Fashion-Week, Allison Palmer. My favourite client and Queen Bee's sartorial saviour of last resort, Allison Palmer. Allison Palmer, who was going to save us from sinking into small business oblivion. Allison Palmer, who was going to guarantee us the success necessary to sail into the next twelve months still financially afloat. Kurt would have to fend for himself because this was more important than finding his place card.

Now, I'm a glass-half-full kinda girl. I like to always look on the bright side; I say 'can' when others say 'can't'; and I can find a silver lining in any cloud. But as I stood watching that she-devil charm Allison that night I knew it could mean only one thing: Diane was trying to poach my client. This was like Belle Single all over again. Only this time I was determined not to lose. Allison, to her credit, looked decidedly uncomfortable about the whole conversation, shifting awkwardly from one Manolo-clad foot to the other and glancing hopefully over Diane's shoulder as if looking for an escape. And for a moment I toyed with the idea of offering one. I thought about waltzing over, barging into the conversation and shaming Diane for her duplicity. Only, you have to have a conscience in order for it to be shamed and there was the vital flaw in my plan. Diane was sadly lacking in that department. Instead, I stood and watched and vowed that the publicity campaign we delivered for Allison at BMW Australian Fashion Week would blow her sequinned socks off so she'd simply have no reason to switch publicists.

That *and* I grabbed another glass of champagne even though my first glass was still far from empty.

'Thirsty?' asked the suit standing beside me.

I smiled half-heartedly. I didn't recognise this guy as press and I certainly wasn't going to waste my energy being polite to anyone else. A swagger of *Coco* finalists wandered past, escaped from the green room and easily identified by their magazine rosettes.

The suit leaned in. 'Those guys only have one look, for Christ's sake! Blue Steel? Ferrari? Le Tigre? They're all the same face.'

I laughed despite myself. 'And who might you be? Not a finalist this evening, I take it?'

The suit stuck out his hand. 'Michael Lloyd. Pleased to meet you.'

'Michael Lloyd!' I exclaimed excitedly. 'We're sitting at the same table!' This was my knight in shining Armani. My saviour in Paul Smith. Michael Lloyd was the only person at my table I wouldn't pay a hit man to take out.

'Great,' he enthused. 'You must know my girlfriend, then?'

Warning lights flashed before my eyes.

'Belle Single,' he added, by way of explanation.

Belle. Bloody. Single.

'Belle Single?' I said weakly. He was Belle Single's latest squeeze? That made him the reason my media conference fell flat, I thought, resolving to hate Michael Lloyd forevermore with immediate effect. I took a long swig of champagne.

Thank God Lulu chose this moment to interrupt us. Skittering across the ballroom floor, she skidded to a stop in front of me. 'Er, Jasmine, can we borrow you for a minute backstage?'

I didn't need to be asked twice. 'Sorry, Michael. Duty calls and all that. I've got to run and – er, what do I need to run and do?' I asked Lulu.

'Our stylist won't style and I don't know what to do!' she wailed.

I grimaced, embarrassed in front of Michael. 'Uh, I'll catch you at dinner,' I said, grabbing Lulu by the arm and walking her away at speed. 'What do you mean, the stylist won't style?' I hissed. 'What's he here for? The ambiance?'

Lulu just shrugged.

Backstage, I saw exactly what she meant. The stylist wouldn't style.

In fact, not only would he not style tonight. Turned out our Vidal Sassoon didn't style, full stop. Not ever. Didn't get his manicured hands dirty with anything more demanding than 'supervising', apparently.

'Bud, I don't know who the hell you think you are,' I screeched, 'but I've got forty bachelors with flat hair here. So either you attach yourself to a blowdryer or I'll do that for you!'

Heads everywhere snapped to look in our direction. None of them bloody styled, of course.

Our rebellious barber didn't budge.

'Look, big shot, let me explain how it works around here. You're a stylist? You style. Do you think I'm too good to do PR? Do you think I just supervise my publicists? Hell, no. I put my issues in my pocket and get on with it. I call the press. I write the press releases. Heck, in my workplace, I even change the toilet paper rolls. Now, *style*!'

Just then Samantha Priest sauntered past, all Botox and boobs and blonde hair (and no sign of Doctor Fun), and interrupted my tirade. 'Jesus, Jazzy, keep your shirt on or you'll end up back in Emergency. The blokes are the only ones we want to see topless tonight, yeah?'

All class as usual. I swear, that girl gave bogans a bad name.

Just then I spied Leila Graham entering the green room. Tonight's event was Leila's baby and she was understandably very nervous.

'You're gunna be blown away by this evening, Leila!' I reassured her. 'The results will be *incred*, I promise you!'

Leila smiled tightly. Despite all our hard work on this campaign, I could tell that the disastrous media call at the Beresford was not far from her mind.

'Have you seen the number of press out there?' I indicated to the jam-packed ballroom. Leila nodded. Another grim smile. Nothing I could possibly say would help; I just had to make sure I delivered the goods. Promising to check in regularly throughout the night, I left Leila biting her nails and teetered back to my table, where I steeled myself for the worst.

Ever seen that *Absolutely Fabulous* episode where Patsy declares it the right season for funerals? Consoling the bereaved, she declares, 'Well, Harvey Nicks have got some really tasty little black numbers at the moment. Black is like, in. You wouldn't have to wear it only the once.' I felt I should have dressed in black that evening like the rest of my Queen Bee team. Because what I endured throughout the Coco Man of the Year Awards certainly felt a lot like my funeral. Instead, however, I was clad head to toe in shiny, sparkling sequins. But tonight my Ellery ensemble left me feeling like a disco ball. A dazzling, glittering disco ball. A disco ball saying: 'Kick me.'

MICHAEL: So who's going to walk away with the prize tonight? Any bets?

AMANDA: What are we wagering?

BELLE SINGLE (as a particularly burly bunch of AFL players walk by): I'll bet anything.

ME (incredulously): Did you say you'll bed anything?

DIANE: What is it with you and sportsmen, Jasmine? Try to refrain while I'm eating. You know it puts me off my food.

ME: I didn't realise you were eating again.

DIANE (looking me up and down): Yes, unlike some.

MICHAEL (gallantly intervening): So the Man of the Year, any picks?

BELLE SINGLE: Hmm, and we can only have one?

ME: (Insert tongue-biting here.)

MICHAEL: Yes, just one. That's the idea.

AMANDA: Can I still bet if I know the winner?

ME: Sure, because everything you know is strictly confidential.

AMANDA: Now you tell me.

DIANE: My, that's a tight ship you're running, Jasmine.

ME (seething): I find I lose less people overboard that way.

DIANE: Oh, really? That's not what I've heard. Word on the street is your favourite client is looking to jump ship . . .

MICHAEL (to the rescue yet again): How 'bout I top up your glass there, sailor?

ME: Please. You know you'd make a fine first mate?

MICHAEL (winking): Aye, aye, cap'n.

BELLE SINGLE (hissing so only I can hear): Flirt like that again, Jasmine Lewis, and I'll sink you.

SOME POOR SCHMUCK UNLUCKY ENOUGH TO BE SEATED AT OUR TABLE: Can someone pass the bread please?

ME: Bread? There's no bread here. Haven't you been to a fashion function before?

BELLE SINGLE (incongruously): I'd like that dreamy Kurt Simmons to win.

DIANE (maliciously): Kurt Simmons? The dull-as-dishwater, squeaky-clean Kurt Simmons? Why, yes, I'd be interested to see Kurt win, too.

AMANDA: OMG, can you imagine! What a PR nightmare! I'd rather watch my Tuscan spray tan dry than read an interview with Kurt Simmons. I'll die if he wins.

ME: Don't you get anything right? Kurt Simmons does win, you imbecile!

Actually, that's not quite true. What I *really* said was: 'Oh, I don't know, Amanda. I think it would be a great professional challenge to try and make Kurt Simmons newsworthy.'

Diane smirked. Amanda looked sceptical. Belle Single just looked confused.

By the time the winner's announcement rolled around, the evening already felt endless. Years of my life had passed since my chauffeur dropped me off at the foot of the red carpet earlier this evening. I'd had relationships that had lasted less time. In fact, if Michael hadn't been there that night, refilling my glass and removing the knives from my back, I would have retreated to the green room long ago. Who knew Belle Single could have such good taste in men? I guess she'd stuck enough in her mouth over the years to finally find the right flavour. Although she looked suspiciously like she was ready for a new taste right now, as we watched the bachelors traipse on stage. Seriously, the girl was in danger of drooling on her Proenza dress.

But Single's slobber was the least of my worries when the *Coco* Man of the Year was announced that night.

The lights were dimmed, a spotlight was raised. A line-up of made-up metrosexuals held their breath. Then, slowly, painstakingly, Leila Graham stepped to the microphone and prised open *that* envelope.

'The women of Australia have spoken,' she declared.

The media in the room closed in.

'The winner . . .'

Journalists were poised.

'. . . of the *Coco* Man of the Year Award . . .'

Film crews strained forward.

'. . . is . . .'

Snappers jostled for position.

'. . . Kurt Simmons!'

Amanda gasped in surprise.

Kurt smiled graciously.

Diane smiled ungraciously.

And press everywhere sighed in dismay.

As thunderous applause echoed round the Ivy and the impeccable Kurt shook hands politely with his competitors, disappointed journalists began to pack up their news crews and head for the bar. 'Kurt Simmons?' said one disgusted hack near me. 'How am I supposed to fill a column with Kurt Simmons?' Their deflation was palpable.

All, that is, except for one audacious intern.

'Kurt! Kurt, over here. Tara Robinson, Channel Six *Nightly News*. How does it feel to be named Man of the Year?' She thrust a microphone into Kurt's chiselled but bland face and watched as cardboard words tumbled out of his mouth. I had to hand it to her, she had chutzpah. Only, had no one told her this was a CCP event? A CCP event that was proudly sponsored, nay, wholly owned, by CCP's good mates and Channel Six's rival, Network Twelve? Tara Robinson wasn't going to win friends and influence people by gazumping Network Twelve at their own event. Someone oughta tell this kid she wasn't in Kansas any more.

Oblivious, she doggedly hunted down her scoop.

Suddenly, just like in Judy Garland's glorious film, my world turned from technicolour to ominous black and white: the Head of Channel Twelve stood towering before me. Her face was grey with rage.

This could not be good.

'What the hell is going on?' she asked me. 'Why the fuck is some hack from Six getting our Man of the Year exclusive? Didn't I pay for this event? Isn't it my name on your pay cheque?'

My jaw dropped in astonishment.

'Well?' she screamed.

The room fell silent. My dress sparkled loudly.

'Why the hell isn't that us?' She pointed to the stage, where Tara was chatting blithely to Kurt while her film crew diligently got a close-up of his award. 'Well?' she shrieked again.

I twinkled in reply.

Journalists flocked from all corners of the room, Kurt Simmons' stud status quickly overshadowed by our brawl. The light from dozens of digital cameras bouncing off my sequins was blinding.

'What the hell is Six doing there?'

'Channel Six is just showing some initiative,' I answered boldly. 'While I made sure there was a Network Twelve crew here tonight, I can't dictate what they film. It seems your crew simply wasn't up to speed.'

Crickets chirped loudly. Someone at a nearby table cleared their throat. The cameras rolled jubilantly on.

'Wasn't. Up. To. Speed?' the network head echoed, her voice barely audible. I swear the Wicked Witch of the West had nothing on this woman.

'That's right,' I said, confidently. 'What do you expect me to do? Jump on stage and accost Tara Robinson? Crash-tackle her off the podium? Your crew had every opportunity to get up there and interview Kurt for themselves. Like I said, I guess they simply weren't fast enough.'

And with that, she lunged at me.

'Gah!' I yelped as I jumped out of her way, sending a nearby waitress sprawling.

Snappers went berserk and I sparkled like a disco ball in their midst.

'How dare you –' my assailant yelled and I braced myself for round two.

As I jostled around in the media scrum, security muscled in and attempted to drag the network chief out.

'Get your hands off me!' she shrieked. 'I own this event!' The beefy bouncers stopped in their tracks.

'Look,' I declared, 'when I was hired to get publicity, you never specified with which network.' I ducked behind the bouncers. 'And anyway,' I added, safely on the right side of security, 'I think you just earned us tomorrow's headlines.'

Just because you call a show *Australia's Got Talent* doesn't mean we do. Much like *Keeping Up with the Kardashians* doesn't require much mental exertion. And *The Hills* doesn't feature much landscape. But in naming my company Queen Bee PR, I could honestly promise clients exactly what it said on the tin. Because the media coverage we scored for the Coco Man of the Year Awards really was fit for a queen. It was royally huge. We're talking truly majestic stuff.

Following my altercation with the head of Network Twelve, the Coco event enjoyed a significant slot on the late-night news, my sparkly Ellery number bumping even a football scandal from top billing. Surely my finest career moment to date. This coverage was closely followed by the front page of the *Sun* the next day, under the banner heading CATFIGHT DOGS BACHELOR PARTY. Not to mention a decent-sized column in the *Advertiser*, replete with colour images of our brawl. By eight in the morning we were the number one trending topic on Twitter, and by nine we were the talk of talkback radio. Ten saw us score two morning TV mentions and by lunchtime the office phone was ringing off the hook. By 2 pm Coco's bumper bachelor edition was walking off the shelves, but it was only when I heard from Leila at 3 pm that I finally breathed a sigh of relief.

As the media clippings piled up on my desk, Lulu struggled into my office weighed down by an enormous bunch of flowers. I whipped off the card and slit open the envelope. The message inside? *Jazzy Lou, With you, all publicity really is good publicity. Thanks for the ink, Leila.*

'We did it!' I shouted to the Bees, who came buzzing from all corners of the office when they heard my excited screeching. 'Coco love us! We did it!' Now all we had to do was back it up with BMW Australian Fashion Week. Simple, right?

With that my phone buzzed with a call from Allison Palmer. 'I'm so sorry, love,' she gushed apologetically without giving me a chance to get a word in. 'I know you saw me talking to Diane last night. The thing is,' she rushed on, 'my sales agent is on my case about growing the business and if I don't wow them at Fashion Week she wants me to think seriously about changing publicity companies. It's nothing personal. And you know if it was just me I'd never leave you. But I've got my employees to consider . . .' Allison trailed off.

Nothing personal? My favourite client was considering dumping me for the devil incarnate and I was not meant to take it personally?

I paused before responding. I knew this wasn't Allison's doing. I knew she was under pressure from her agent (and that the conniving Diane would have played no small part in adding to that pressure). But I couldn't pretend it didn't hurt.

'Look, babe,' I answered finally. 'I know how important this Fashion Week is to you. I know it really is make or break for you at this point in your career. But let's not even talk about switching teams until you've seen what the Bees can deliver for you because I promise you won't be disappointed.'

'Oh, Jazzy Lou, I believe in you!' she said and I knew she really meant it.

For the sake of Queen Bee PR, I just hoped that I did too.

18

Osama bin Laden was dead. This was the worst news I'd received since the World Health Organization linked mobile phone usage to brain cancer. Not that I didn't want the man six feet under, but the timing of his demise couldn't have been worse.

You see, bin Laden bid farewell on the eve of Allison Palmer's show at BMW Australian Fashion Week.

And while to even put the two in the same sentence might sound flippant, consider this: Allison Palmer's show cost close to forty thousand dollars to produce and would inject many times that much into the local economy. An economy still recovering from the GFC. It was employing countless people, from models to musicians, from stylists to sound technicians. Plus, this really was the show to launch Allison's much-deserved career. Not to mention make or break mine.

If only I could convince the press to cover it.

But on the day of Allison's catwalk show the *Sun* newspaper – the front page of which was supposed to be sporting the new face of fashion – was now plastered with the old guard of al-Qaeda.

'OMG! I can't believe bin Laden is dead,' said Lulu, holding up a complimentary copy of the *Sun* from where it lay on a front-row seat ahead of Allison's catwalk show. *'What* an ugly photo to have on the front page for Fashion Week!'

I couldn't help but think President Obama would disagree. Still, the US President was about the only person who *wasn't* at BMW Fashion Week. As if to prove my point, a certain makeup king minced past in his crocodile-skin shoes and Gucci sunglasses, a gaggle of adoring fans in his wake.

It was not even 7 am at the Sydney Harbour Overseas Passenger Terminal, the style centre of Sydney for the next week, but the Bees and I had already been hard at it for hours. The catwalk for Allison's collection had been laid last night, after the previous show had finished. So now we traipsed up and down the plastic-covered runway toting gift bags that weighed more than your average catwalk model.

'Remember, no stilettos allowed on the runway,' I yelled at no one in particular. 'So either walk down the gutter or take your shoes off altogether.' There was no need to mention the third, impossible option: wear flats. This was Fashion Week, baby, and heels were de rigueur. At the end of the catwalk a svelte violinist in six-inch heels tuned up her electric violin as she prepared to accompany this morning's models down the runway. As her fingers moved like quicksilver down the neck of her instrument, the dramatic melodies of Vivaldi were born with heart-breaking purity. Momentarily, at least.

'Stop!' I shouted, her amplified strings no match for my voice box. 'Someone Blixz her fingernails now! Are Blixz today's sponsors or what?' Seriously. What was wrong with everyone here?

Stalking to the back of the show space, I began to inspect the scaffolding set up for the press photographers. Three tiers of viewing platforms stood before me with laminated plastic signs gaffer-taped to the floor, staking out all the prime positions. AVP newswire, Hallsdorf, Leah McSeen Photography, Style TV, Vicktor Hugo Press, Channel Twelve, the Sun, Channel Six. Anyone who was anyone was represented. I just hoped they'd show.

A parade of pouty Fashion Week volunteers skulked past me. These girls were young enough to make Justin Bieber look like a paedophile but their Taylor Momsen makeup belied their age. 'Right, all vollies over here,' someone official addressed them. 'You lot will be dressing and you lot will be ushers. If you're dressing, get backstage now.'

The girls assigned to dressing the models in their outfits for the show swaggered backstage. The ushers were ushered to the foyer, where they hung around awaiting further direction and enviously eyed the promo girls dressed as old-school cinema usherettes giving away alcopops at the door. Such is the hierarchy of minions.

As the lights were dimmed for a full dress rehearsal, and the cleaners brought in for a final scrub of the show space, I headed out to the car park to the hair and makeup marquee to check our models were behaving. It was still too early for me to hit the phones to the press and try to recover some of the media coverage that had been annihilated overnight, so I had to settle for double-triple-checking that every other detail was perfect for this morning's show.

'Make sure all handles are on the *outside* of the gift bags,' I hollered to the Bees as I left the show area. An instruction they'd each received a thousand times before. I was debating whether to head back in and check the girls were doing it right when I bumped into Anya in the foyer.

'Jazzy Lou, you'll never guess what I have for you!' she exclaimed. We were standing in the grand entrance to Fashion Week, surrounded by giant TV screens blaring urgent Facebook updates while rolling tweets ran along the bottom of the screen.

'What?' Unless it was a front-page headline featuring Allison Palmer's name, I was going to be disappointed.

Anya smiled mysteriously.

And then she did the last thing in the entire world I expected. She produced a battered old Louis Vuitton Speedy handbag. My battered old Louis Vuitton Speedy handbag. The same handbag that had been stolen from my car all that time ago.

'I found it in Oxford Street Vinnies!' she announced triumphantly.

I was mortified. 'Gah! Are you for real? What the hell were you doing in Vinnies?' I exclaimed. St Vincent de Paul's? Op-shopping? That's so not kosher.

Anya rolled her eyes. 'Aren't you pleased to have it back?'

I paused. Here I was in the midst of Australian Fashion Week, preparing for a forty-thousand-dollar catwalk show and perhaps my biggest event to date. Sure, the media might be in meltdown and press coverage was going to be scarcer than real breasts in the Eastern Suburbs, but nothing had actually gone wrong *yet*. Hell, we might even make it a Queen Bee success. And you know what? I *was* pleased to have my Speedy back. If only because it reminded me of how very far I'd come. Working at Wilderstein PR felt like a distant memory when I held that Speedy in my hands.

'Thanks, love. It's *amaze*,' I said genuinely to Anya. 'But how on earth do you even know it's the same Speedy I lost?'

Anya laughed. 'Recognise these?' She tipped the bag upside down and pointed to smeary blood-red marks staining the leather on the bottom of the bag.

'OMG! It *is* my Speedy! Do you remember that day Diane threw an open bottle of OPI nail polish at my head?' I shuddered as the memory came flooding back.

'Monsooner or Later,' Anya grimaced, recalling the exact shade. 'Thank God you had your Speedy handy or you might still be removing Monsooner from your pores.'

'I wonder if the bag's still got Raven's red knickers stashed inside,' I joked and went to peer into the Speedy when two skinny, pale models wandered by, looking like albino giraffes. Wait a minute. Pale models? Not at my show.

'Are you two walking for Allison Palmer?' I snapped.

The giraffes nodded.

'Then where's your spray tan?' I exploded. 'Get backstage and get tanned now!'

The giraffes scampered.

'I've got to run and sort this,' I apologised to Anya. 'This is diabolical.' Thanking her again for finding my handbag, I slipped it onto my arm and headed out to the hair and makeup marquee.

The scene that greeted me resembled a zoo.

Even though it was not yet 8 am, the small synthetic hothouse of the makeup marquee was pumping. Condensation trickled down the clear plastic walls, and when I prised open the door to the tent, a wave of hairspray hit me. This was followed by a wall of noise. Inside was a barrage of stylists, hairdressers, makeup artists and models, all talking over the top of one another, while music blared in the background and mounted TV screens screamed to be heard. There were feathers, fur, leather and sequins. And, of course, mirrors on every available surface.

Poking my head into the madness, I breathed deeply and then let rip: 'If you're on my catwalk today,' I bellowed, 'then you'd better be looking orange. And if you're not, get backstage and get yourself a spray tan now!' I slammed the door for added emphasis. The plastic reverberated in my hand.

Turning on my heels, I stalked towards backstage to start the first of my media calls for the day; this was when the real animal taming would begin.

If the makeup room was a zoo then backstage was a circus.

Rows of clothing rails stood at the entry, welcoming guests to the three rings inside. I pulled back the theatrical red velvet curtain to reveal the madness within. Waiflike models lounged around in their lingerie, bones protruding and eyes staring vacantly, their

IQs apparently only slightly higher than their BMIs. A waiter wafted past bearing a tray of miniature food. Mini yoghurts, mini muffins, mini croissants, mini Danishes. Never mind supersize, no one in fashion even eats normal-sized. In the corner, one vollie stood steaming garments – a post she never left all day. Alice lay sprawled on the floor, her iPad in one hand, her BlackBerry in the other, uploading images onto the Queen Bee blog. Next to her, like a scene from a hundred years earlier, two women sat sewing sequins by hand onto a spectacular Allison Palmer frock.

It was now only a few short hours till showtime and, like any good ringmaster, I cracked a mean whip.

'Right, there should be three garments on each clothing rail outside,' I yelled. 'Can someone tell me why some rails only have two?'

Someone, somewhere, started to answer.

'Wait – don't tell me,' I interrupted. 'Just fix it.'

'And you vollies.' I pointed. 'I need you to start checking all the garments. Work from left to right along each rail and make sure everything is in order. There'll be no time once the show has started to search for accessories between each look. Unzip all zips now. Check all cuffs. You need to be ready before the first girl hits the runway.'

Eyeliner-wearing tweens scattered in all directions.

'And don't forget there's over one million dollars worth of Jan Logan jewellery back here. Don't. Lose. Anything!' I screamed, before turning my attention to Alice. 'Alice, where's Allison? Have we seen her yet this morning?' Alice shook her head. 'Find out where she is and get her whatever she wants,' I replied before turning my attention to my BlackBerry. It was time to muster some media.

Scrolling through my inbox was diabolically dull. It should have been overflowing with media enquiries but instead I'd had no new emails in nearly half an hour. This was unheard of. It was such a bad day to be chasing press.

I hit Luke's number on speed dial.

'Babe?' he answered groggily.

'I need your help,' I said without preamble. There was no time for niceties, it was nearly 9 am. 'Actually, I need your column inches. I can't get traction anywhere today. There are Seals on the front page of every paper in the country and I've got a circus here with everything but.'

'Huh? Seals? At Fashion Week?' Luke was confused. Clearly, he hadn't heard about Obama's crack team. 'But isn't fur in this season, Jazzy Lou? Surely you can work with that?'

'You don't understand,' I said bluntly. 'I'm here in sequin central for Allison Palmer's show and it's a media moratorium. You've got to come cover the show for me.'

Luke sighed. And made a noise that sounded suspiciously like someone rolling over in bed. 'What time do you need me?' he said finally.

Thank God. 'Be here by 10 am. I owe you big time,' I replied.

'Yes, you do, Jazzy Lou,' Luke signed off. 'Yes you do.'

I knew I could rely on him.

Next I tried the *Chronicle*, the *Courier*, the *Spectator* and the *Star*. I called the *Advertiser*, the *Observer*, the *Leader* and the *Times*. I argued with the *Argus* and I bullied the *Bulletin*. And all without result.

I was beginning to wonder whether Diane had personally arranged for bin Laden to get the bullet, such was the catastrophe it had caused me. God knows, nothing would surprise me about that woman's power to maim or kill.

Leaving no stone unturned, I scrolled to Pamela's name in my contacts list.

'Pamela Stone! My *fave* gossip queen,' I started.

'Sorry, doll, unless you're ringing me about bin Laden, I'm afraid there's no space available today,' said Pamela, preparing to hang up.

'Wait! I am!' I said desperately.

'You *are?*' Pamela didn't even try to disguise her surprise.

'Er, yeah, I am,' I repeated. I thought if I said it enough times it might just be true.

'I'm all ears.'

'So, you know how Osama has died,' I stalled.

'I had heard,' Pamela said dryly.

'Well, er –' I scanned the room for inspiration.

'Yes?'

'Well, you see –' I started again when a volunteer appeared out of nowhere, brandishing my old Speedy handbag.

'Jasmine Lewis! You left your bag in the makeup room!' the vollie yelled.

I took the bag and slipped it over my arm for the second time that morning. This bag was like a bloody boomerang. I was destined never to be permanently parted from it. Or Raven's red knickers, which were probably still floating around inside somewhere.

243

And then it hit me.

Raven's knickers! Actually, any celebrity's knickers. This was just what we needed. Knickers. Famous knickers. And hats and shoes and frocks and toenail clippings, for all I cared. Anything, as long as its owner was famous. This idea was inspired. Raven's red g-string might save my arse yet.

'Well, Pamela, we're hosting a celebrity auction at Allison Palmer's catwalk show here at Fashion Week today. All proceeds are going to the families of the New York Fire Department. Because we don't want those poor people to be forgotten now that the hunt for bin Laden is over.'

'So you're auctioning celebrity memorabilia?' Pamela asked. 'Like what?'

That was a good question. It was 9.23 am. The first model was due to walk at 11 am. And I had no celebrity memorabilia to speak of. Clearly, I would not be auctioning celebrity memorabilia that morning. Better think fast.

'No, no, Pamela. We're not auctioning celebrity *stuff*,' I said. 'No, nothing as crass as that. God, the last thing I want to do is make our celeb clientele feel like exhibits in a zoo. No, we're hosting an auction for celebrities to *participate* in. Wave some paddles around. You know, bid, darling. All of the gorgeous gowns in Allison Palmer's show will be going under the hammer immediately following the event. And all of our special front-row guests are invited to bid. Because nothing feels as good as owning a haute couture piece, does it?'

There was silence on the line. Then: 'Doll, that is a simply *gorge* idea. I love it. What time do you kick off? I'll have the car brought around now. And you must save me a seat in the front row! Ta ta.'

Boom! What a result! Sydney's social pages sovereign was going to cover our event.

I just hoped like hell Allison would be okay with my plan. But I couldn't see why not. The gowns she was showing were only samples, after all. And the publicity of having a celeb bid for your designs would be worth so much more than any frock itself. Plus, at least this way I was auctioning something I actually *had*. (Even if it wasn't mine to sell.) A slightly better scenario than selling celebrity memorabilia I didn't have, non?

So now all I had to do was organise and promote a charity auction. In a little less than two hours. I instinctively reached for my Nurofen, then I remembered. Of *course*. I'd been blacklisted. Ever since my local pharmacy had got wind of my Nurofen-induced stomach ulcer they'd chalked me up as a crack-whore-ice-addict, the kind of lowlife who probably tested her cosmetics on innocent bunnies each morning and who willing gives E-numbers to children. The result? Now my overzealous chemist would sell me nothing stronger than a herbal remedy. I grabbed the small floral-scented spritzer from my bag and poured its contents down my throat, swallowing a bouquet of bush herbs whole.

'Not liposuction. Celeb *auction*!' I had to shout to be heard over the din of hairdryers. 'Like, fundraising for the less fortunate and stuff!'

Only Shelley could think 10 am on a weekday morning – and a weekday morning during Fashion Week, no less – was a good time for a nip and tuck.

'But I'm flattered you thought I was calling from your surgeon's rooms,' I added sarcastically, without pausing to ask what exactly she thought I was having done. That was one can of weight-loss leeches that didn't need opening. Instead I said, 'I need you to source some auction paddles for me, Shell.'

The clock was ticking and it was all hands on deck if we were ever going to get to smashing champagne over the bow of this auction. I already had Allison pricing her stock and the Bees designing a buyers' guide to be handed to all A-list guests at the show. Myself, I was just shooting off a press release to every outlet and contact I knew when the camera crew from Network Six appeared backstage for their prearranged interview with Allison. This was one interview I'd managed to hang on to and simply by not being too proud to beg. The fact that I'd nearly come to blows with Channel Twelve – their main rival – at the Coco Awards hadn't hurt my standing at Six either.

'Welcome!' I bellowed, stepping over sequin-sewing minions and extending a frantic arm. 'Come on in, let me clear some room for you.' I kicked the seamstresses out of the way.

The crew trudged on in.

'And Kate McClelland!' I cried, spotting the petite TV journalist behind them. 'So great to see you!'

Kate offered a warm smile. I could have offered my firstborn in return. At last, some fucking media coverage.

'Please meet our very talented designer, Allison Palmer.' I thrust Allison forward.

Polite introductions all round.

'Now, shall we jump straight in and run through the script?' I suggested. If we could provide enough tasty sound bites, this interview might just eat into both the 4 pm and 6 pm bulletins.

Kate nodded compliantly.

Allison looked petrified.

As the crew set up their cameras, Kate and Allison rehearsed their script while I hovered over them. 'If it's all right with you, I'd like to start by asking: "Why BMW Australian Fashion Week?"' Kate said.

Allison turned to me questioningly.

'Great!' I replied. 'And Allison's answer is: "As a born and bred Sydneysider, there's no runway I'd prefer a run at!"'

Kate nodded approvingly. 'That's great,' she said. 'We're only broadcasting in the Sydney major metro area so there's no require-ment to pacify Melbourne viewers. Shall we film that?'

Allison looked like she might faint.

'Let's,' I replied as the crew bunged on a spotlight behind us.

Kate switched on her on-air persona to match. 'Dust off your Dior and dig out your Dolce & Gabbana, ladies, because today we're broadcasting from backstage at BMW Australian Fashion Week, where I'm speaking with debut designer Allison Palmer. Now Allison, why have you chosen Australian Fashion Week for your very first catwalk show?'

The camera swung around to Allison, who looked impeccable in one of her own flawless creations.

'Well . . .' she started. And then she froze. 'Um, what's the answer again, Jazzy?' she said nervously, still looking down the barrel of the camera. The cameraman sighed and swung the camera off his shoulder. Kate smiled graciously and we began over again from the top.

Lining up for a second take, Kate posed the question thoughtfully, as if it had only just popped into her mind: 'Now Allison, why have you chosen Australian Fashion Week for your very first catwalk show?'

But just as Allison prepared to answer, a courier bumped into the room, wheeling a squeaky clothing rail behind him and shouting for a signatory for his delivery.

'Gah!' I screamed. 'We're filming here, people! Channel Six News! Very important!'

The cameraman puffed out his chest. The racket behind me carried on. This would never do.

'Everybody shut up! Shut up!' I exploded. 'I don't care who you are and I don't care what you're doing! We're filming a TV interview here that will pay your fashionista wages. No one makes any further noise until I say.'

Silence fell across the room.

The cameraman whistled through his teeth. 'Can we take you with us on all our shoots?' he asked in hushed tones.

I grinned.

Kate started over, unperturbed. 'Dust off your Dior and dig out your Dolce & Gabbana, ladies, because today we're broadcasting from backstage at BMW Australian Fashion Week, where I'm speaking with debut designer Allison Palmer —'

'No!' I interrupted. 'That won't do. Allison, you were moving your arms.'

Kate looked bemused. 'That's fine. Arms are fine. They make her look human.'

'She's not allowed to be human,' I explained. 'She's got me next to her.'

Allison swallowed nervously.

Behind me, at that very second, our seamstresses finished work on the showstopper of today's event: a stunning silver ballgown, figure-hugging with a fishtail finish and covered with thousands of sparkling sequins.

'Oh, wow!' exclaimed Kate, spying the dress.

Allison smiled shyly. 'Do you want to take a look? It weighs over eleven kilograms with all those sequins.'

I held the dress up for Kate to admire.

'Wow!' she said again. 'Eleven kilograms? That must be half your weight, Jazzy,' she joked.

I didn't disagree. Stress, it turns out, is not a four-square meal.

Then, turning back to the camera, Kate began her spiel again as I hovered nearby, supervising. After all, if I wasn't there to make sure Allison Palmer was 'on brand' for the Allison Palmer brand, who would? Thankfully Allison looked a little more comfortable now she'd had a chance to show off her work.

'Dust off your Dior and dig out your Dolce & Gabbana, ladies because today we're broadcasting from backstage at BMW Australian Fashion Week, where I'm speaking with debut designer Allison Palmer . . .'

Out in the foyer, meawhile, where the Moët bubbled and the Gucci glittered, A-listers began to amass. They flittered about ethereally, their faces at once recognisable yet at the same time representing something tantalisingly out of reach. The paparazzi snapped at their well-shod heels. The glitterati were out in full force.

There was Samantha Priest, her long hair extensions glistening in the morning sunshine bouncing off the harbour. There was Pamela Stone, her regal presence filling the packed room while her eyes scanned for tomorrow's headline. There was the blonde bombshell Belle Single, batting her lashes for the panting paps. And oh! beside her was the handsome Michael Lloyd, I couldn't help but notice. There was racing royalty Sara Goldbridge, her long legs looking more elongated than ever, as if designed to mock her mother's prized jockeys. There were ubiquitous reality TV stars. There were celebrated television chefs. There were famous radio hosts and there were infamous football stars. There were shoe doyennes and there were millinery masters. There were fashion muses and there were fashion slaves. Plus, there were fashion editors aplenty.

And there, in the thick of things, was Luke.

'OMG, sweetie,' he cried to the Botoxed beauty beside him who was embalmed in new-season Versace. 'Did you hear Cate Blanchett will be here at Allison's show? Word on the street is she's going to bid on the final gown, so I'd put in an advance bid if I were you. But that's strictly confidential, babe,' he added, winking then swanning off to the next cluster of celebs.

I caught his eye and flashed him a winning smile. Mazel tov, my friend. Mazel tov.

Then, without warning, I felt a bump from behind, followed by the unmistakable fizz of champagne hitting my exposed skin. 'Oops!' cried a familiar voice. I spun around, spraying droplets of Moët on everyone in my vicinity, and found myself face to face with Belle bloody Single. 'I tripped!' she added, as if that explained the river of sparkling wine flowing down my back and into the waistline of my backless Oscar de la Renta number.

I raised a sceptical eyebrow. 'You tripped? And lost the entire contents of your champagne flute on my Ciao Bella spray tan?' Diabolical! If this hadn't been my own event I would have caused one hell of a scene right now. I wasn't even sure I wouldn't. What the hell had I done to deserve this? Other than flirting outrageously with her boyfriend all night at the Coco Man of the Year Awards, that is.

Belle smirked, her artificially white teeth the purest thing about her.

Two could play this game.

'Oh, Michael!' I called, spotting Belle's beau engrossed in conversation a few steps behind her. 'Could I borrow you for a minute? Sadly your girlfriend seems to have lost her drink. No, she doesn't need another. But I could use a hand mopping it up, please?' I turned my naked and now dripping-wet back to Michael.

His jaw dropped. Belle scowled. And I smiled as Michael very graciously helped me dry off.

I was just beginning to enjoy myself when I spied Diane across the room, her giant Dior sunglasses shielding innocent bystanders from the laser beams of hate she shot in my direction. I smiled sweetly in response. Much as having Belle Single's boyfriend wipe down my naked back was fun, nothing would give me greater pleasure today than to wipe the floor with Diane.

Then the doors to the show space swung open and the dance of the beautiful people began in earnest. A-list celebrities glided graciously to the front row, obliging the snappers who pursued them on the way. There was Ruby Rose and Christine Centenera and Jodhi Meares and Dannii Minogue. Erin McNaught was there and John Ibrahim too. Russell Crowe wandered by, Danielle Spencer on his arm, as Laura Dundovic and Sophie Monk hunted for their seats. There was Justin Hemmes, Tom Williams, Nat Bassingthwaighte and Joel Christie. There was small screen queen Kerri-Anne Kennerley, plus Lisa Wilkinson, Melissa Doyle, Kylie Gillies, Yumi Stynes and Carrie Bickmore. Even Jessica Mauboy made an appearance, as did Kyle and Jackie O.

Next the B-listers burst in, all pursed lips and hands on hips, posing for the waiting press. Then came our C-list clientele, shipped in to fill the remaining seats. (One of them immediately fell drunkenly from the back row of tiered seating, clearly unused to free alcohol. *And that's why you're in the back row, sweetie*, I thought, exasperated. *Well, that and the fact you're a little on the tubby side.*) As I raced backstage, the tiers of press photographers filled up too. As did the press section. We just might pull this off, I thought as the pink-haired fashion editor of *Muse* slipped in, looking cool as fuck. Then, hot on her heels, came Shelley decked out in Derek Lam and brandishing bidding paddles. Spotting my head poking out from backstage, she waved the paddles wildly, sending the old queens next to her into an early bidding frenzy.

'Jazzy Lou!' she shouted, struggling to be heard over the pumping pre-show music.

'You are *beyond!*' I replied, racing forward to retrieve the paddles. 'But where on earth did you get these?'

Shelley grinned. 'It's amazing what you can buy on eBay these days.' She winked as she returned to her seat.

I didn't know what was more incredible: Shelley buying bidding paddles on eBay in only a couple of hours, or Shelley buying bidding paddles on eBay full stop.

Schlepping back behind the scenes, I had just enough time to join Allison for a last-minute check of our models before the house lights were dimmed. Emma, who was standing nearby, held up her crossed fingers for me and Allison to see. Through gritted teeth I whispered nervously, 'If we pull this off, I'll eat my hat.' Em smiled encouragingly. Silence descended. And our first model, as they say, stepped forward to break a leg.

Only she didn't.

Break a leg, that is. Oh, no. Instead, our first leggy model stepped onto the catwalk to the strains of Vivaldi and to spontaneous, wondrous applause. Rapturous applause. Thunderous applause. Arse-saving, career-making applause. Applause that caused Em to turn and point to an invisible hat on her head and wink. Applause that I would *happily* eat my hat for. Hell, for applause like this I would have willingly eaten carbs again.

As the first model strode down the runway, shoulders thrown

back and hipbones thrust forward, her sequins sparkled, her pout pouted and the audience lapped it up.

'This is *beyond!*' squealed Allison.

And it really, truly was. I'd never before seen a response like this to a debut catwalk show. Allison had done an amazing job, and the two of us clutched each other in disbelief as a second then a third model joined the first down the runway. The paparazzi papped, fashion editors looked rapt, and beneath her Botoxed veneer, Diane's supercilious smile collapsed. I grinned like a madwoman.

When Lady Gaga received a text from Anna Wintour to say she'd won the Fashion Icon Award at the CFDA Fashion Awards, Gaga thought the message was from a different Anna in her contacts list. Her reply? *Yes, bitch, we did it.* While I, unlike Gaga, stopped short of sending a shout-out to Nuclear Wintour that day, when Allison joined her models on the catwalk for a well-deserved lap of honour I couldn't help but think, *Yes, bitch, we did it.* We really did it. All the hard work, all the sleepless nights, all the obstacles in our way, and the Bees and I had still delivered a successful show, to rapturous applause, in front of a full house of influencers and photographers. This was one for the haters.

Now, if only we could say the same for our last-ditch charity pitch.

Again the house lights dimmed and the spotlight snapped on as a lone skinny model stepped cautiously onto the runway as if stepping out onto a high wire.

The room was silent. The model swayed.

Her sky-blue gown glistened and she took another tentative step forward before halting, balanced in the limelight.

And then? Nothing.

Not a sound.

My career hung in the balance.

You know, it's strange. Very strange. When we've talked about that auction in the years since, reliving every agonising moment, Shelley, Luke and I have never been able to agree on what happened next.

Shelley maintains she was first on her feet, with a wild wave of her paddle and a bold opening bid: 'Five thousand, dah-ling! Six if the dress bloody fits me!' Of course, Shelley walked away that day with enough sequins to clad a small disco-loving third-world nation so she may well have been the one who got the bidding started.

But I beg to differ. From where I stood peering nervously out from backstage, I know I saw Michael Lloyd look squarely in my direction, shake off Belle Single's restraining arm and make an audacious bid. I'm absolutely sure of it. Why else would Belle have looked like all her prospects for social-climbing success had just gone down the toilet?

As for Luke, well, he swears I'm biased. And that as early as that fateful auction day I've only had eyes for Michael Lloyd. Which is a shame, really. As apparently I missed seeing Diane throw up her hands in disgust and storm from the auction room (unwittingly purchasing the item under the hammer at the time). In hindsight, it seems only fair that Diane should donate to my cause. After all, I as good as worked for charity for her all those years.

From there, of course, none of us can argue about what happened next. After all, who could forget the bidding bedlam that ensued? Arms flew in the air as, jewellery jangling, Sydney's glamorous glitterati threw itself behind our cause.

'Boom!' I shrieked to Allison as an ivory micro-dress sold for a macro price.

'OMG!' she screamed at me when a full-length jumpsuit caused a jump in bidding.

'Yes, bitch, we did it!' we squealed in unison as bidding on her amazing silver showstopper stopped the hearts of accountants the city over.

Bitch, we really did it.

When the headlines hit the next day, Allison Palmer was hotter news than Pippa Middleton's arse. FROCK AUCTION STEALS SHOW, screamed the Sun. FASHIONISTA FUNDRAISER RAISES MORE THAN JUST HEM LINES, shouted the Advertiser. And my personal favourite? JAZZY'S CHARITY'S THE BEES' KNEES!

Our fundraiser, it seemed, satisfied the 'good news' criteria of a world-weary Sydney press. And so our feel-good Fashion Week fundraiser filled the closing minutes of the television news on every Sydney station. And as press clippings continued to land in my inbox that day, my phone lit up with Luke's name.

'Luke Jefferson, my favourite hack. What can I do for you, babe?'

Luke laughed. 'Is your life such a whirlwind, Jazzy Lou, that you've forgotten yesterday already, sweetie?' he joked. 'You owe me so much I don't even know where to start.' He laughed even harder at the prospect.

'Sure, shoot,' I said.

'Lunch,' was his reply. 'Some slippery orange fish and a passionfruit caprioska, please.'

'No can do, I'm afraid,' I apologised, even though he must have known it was coming.

'Lemme guess, even after yesterday's coup, you're working through lunch today?'

I sighed. 'You know me too well, Jefferson. I've got a preliminary meeting about an Allison Palmer plaque on The Intersection's Designers Walk of Style in Paddington.'

'That's *incred*, babe,' Luke said genuinely. 'Walk of fame material already? Sheesh, you don't muck around.'

'When you're hot, you're hot.'

'Defs.'

'But I'll tell you what,' I said. 'I'll give you an inside tip for dinner, to make up for missing lunch. If you can get a paparazzo along to Marque restaurant tonight, I promise it will be your lead story tomorrow.'

'Totes?' he asked.

'Totes.'

'And who might be dining at Marque that's so newsworthy?'

I paused. 'Word on the street is Belle Single's boyfriend, Michael Lloyd, is taking another woman out to dinner.'

'No!' Luke cried. 'Who?'

I braced myself for Luke's squeal. 'Moi,' I said.

Sure enough, he screeched down the line, 'Jazzy Lou! You've got a date with Belle Single's beau? *Amaze!*'

I grinned.

'God, no one buries your press conference and gets away with it, do they?' Then he added urgently, 'OMG, what are you going to *wear*?'

I laughed. And then I turned to the Net-a-Porter bag on my desk where inside, so new it still bore its tag, lay one red Vixenary g-string.

Acknowledgements

This book would not have been possible without Felicity McLean — thank you so much for the support and advice during the writing process. To my team of Bettys (aka the Bees) — you make every day possible and without you we would have no stories, no one to pull me into line when I lose my cool and no one to laugh and cry with — daily. I consider you all my sisters, not staff, even when I shout! Thank you to Joel; you are a dear friend and totally inspiring — not to mention a funny bugger. Your support has been endless and I am so grateful. MS . . . thank YOU for the little and not so little tips on where and when Hollywood's hottest celebs hit the tarmac — you have, without question, enabled us to hit the crème de la crème with our brands when our clients thought it would not be humanly possible to get their brands and products on the world's biggest superstars. A huge thank you to Claire, my gorgeous (lipstick-phobic) publisher: I will never forget the day I received your email about doing a book together – and to think where we are now – BEYOND! The hardworking team of sales and marketing gurus who have worked tirelessly on getting Strictly Confidential on the shelves of the best bookstores around the country. To Mum and Dad – it's been a journey and a half and you have provided me with opportunities and guidance that have taken me to where I am today both personally and professionally. When at twenty-four I embarked on the task of starting Sweaty Betty PR you supported me one hundred percent even though you didn't know what PR even was – thank you. To Oli and Little Pixie-Rose . . . I know I am annoying (sometimes), but thank you for putting up with me and my manic work life, odd hours, third arm (BlackBerry) and obsessive compulsive ways – I love you. xRJ